I SPIT
ON YOUR
GRAVES

J'IRAI CRACHER
SUR VOS TOMBES

Boris Vian
(Vernon Sullivan)

TamTam Books

1998

First published in France in 1946
by Editions du Scorpion

English translation by Boris Vian & Milton Rosenthal
first published in France in 1948
by Vendome Préss.

©Christian Bourgois Editeur, 1982.
Introduction by Marc Lapprand © 1998
©1998 TamTam Books

TamTam Books are edited and published by
Tosh Berman.

TamTam Books
2601 Waverly Drive
Los Angeles, CA 90039-2724

tosh@loop.com

First Editon
ISBN 0-9662346-0-X

Library of Congress Catalog Card Number: 97-80958

THE DARK SIDE OF BORIS VIAN

There's a French expression, "secouer le cocotier" (to shake the coconut-tree). The idea is that whoever shakes the coconut-tree secretly hopes that a few coconuts will fall on some heads, not quite accidentally, but in a somewhat random fashion. It may be that Boris Vian was in such a frame of mind when he wrote *J'irai cracher sur vos tombes* in the summer 1946—to shake things up a bit, to get ahead in his life, i.e. to be published. But then little did he know that this B-class thriller would blow up, like a bomb flung into the French literary circus, in the years to come.

How could he foresee that his novel would sell more than half a million copies by 1950, and become the best-seller of 1947, topping all other sales, including those of Sartre, Beauvoir, Camus, and Malraux, the intellectual avant-garde elite of the time.

I Spit On Your Graves was published as if it were the original version of a thriller, written by an African-American writer named Vernon Sullivan. Boris Vian claimed to have translated the novel into French so that it could be published in France. Vian and the publisher explained that the novel's treatment of race was too explosive for it to be published in the U.S.

There was, however, a problem: the original English version was written after the "translation"!

In order for us to understand the multiple literary levels on which this novel works, a brief chronological summary of its publishing life is needed.

At the beginning of the summer of 1946, a young and enterprising publisher wanted a best seller in his catalogue, so that his new publishing company, Editions du Scorpion, could be launched with a big splash. The publisher's name was Jean d' Halluin (brother to the bass-player of the Vian-Abadie Jazz-band). Vian's taste (or veneration) for jazz and thrillers being already well established, d'Halluin approached him, asking him whether he could select a hard-boiled American thriller and translate it for him, for publication by Editions du Scorpion.

Well, Boris Vian decided to write it himself. Why? Perhaps in part to avoid a long search through American thrillers, or maybe just to prove to himself that he could do it.

Things then moved quickly. On his traditional summer vacation with his young family and friends at a beach resort in the Vendée on the Atlantic Coast, Vian wrote the entire novel in the two weeks between August 5th and August 20th. The name of the "author" was chosen: Vernon Sullivan, allegedly made up from the names of his friend Paul Vernon and the jazz pianist Joe Sullivan. The initial title was *J'irai danser sur vos tombes*, "I will dance on your graves," with a clear biblical reference. His wife Michelle thought they needed a grittier title, so they decided that "spit" would serve better than "dance".

J'irai cracher sur vos tombes , "translated" into French by Boris Vian was published in France in November. It was a quiet birth. The book had a slow start. d'Halluin and Vian realized it needed more publicity, otherwise it appeared doomed to sink in the vast sea of print.

They got more than they wanted, in two strokes: one comic, the other more sinister. In February 1947, Daniel Parker, head of a right wing association with the telling name of "Cartel d'action sociale et morale", a group already involved in the moral condemnation of the (in)famous books by Henry Miller, *Tropic of Cancer, Black Spring* , *Tropic of Capricorn* , launched a law suit against the presumed author of *J'irai cracher sur vos tombes* .

Then in April 1947, a sordid murder took place near the Montparnasse Station in Paris. A man went crazy and strangled his mistress in a cheap hotel room. A copy of Vian's thriller was discovered in the murder room. The man who had read it — the murderer — had circled certain passages including the one where Lee Anderson, Vian's hero, strangles Jean Asquith. There was a huge scandal, much to the pleasure of sensation-hungry tabloid readers. Now Vian found himself in a strange and delicate position. Naturally, everybody wanted to read the "murder" book for themselves. So while d'Halluin was busy printing new copies, the unexpected publicity put Vian in the forefront. People wanted to know who the unknown author, Sullivan, was. The situation had become grotesque. The trick had gone too far.

But beyond the publicity, what was so scandalous about *I Spit On Your Graves* ?

The story is narrated by Lee Anderson. He is African-American, but his skin is so light he can pass for white. His younger brother was lynched. Determined to avenge his brother's murder, Lee sets out for Buckton, an imaginary middle-class town in the deep South.

There, through a helpful friend, he secures a quiet job at the bookstore. He mixes confidently with the locals, particularly younger women, whom he ruthlessly exploits and betrays. But he relentlessly seeks the ideal prey upon whom to carry out his planned revenge.

He finds the perfect targets: two women from wealthy families, Lou and Jean Asquith. The plot unfolds at a fast pace. The narrative is incisive, harsh, with few psychological incursions. The story is told mostly through dialogue. As for style — the word "macho" would be too mild. The focus is always on Lee's obsessive determination to kill choice white females. The compensation for the loss of his brother has to be high: two females for one male. He will act without remorse or second thought. But although he can mingle in white society with ease, he believes that his deep voice (he sings the blues) may eventually betray him — he has to act swiftly. The plot is indeed fairly simple and linear, but the story is gripping, the mood is tense. The erotic passages are more suggested than depicted in detail, in a style which Vian himself described as belonging to a "Latin erotic tradition" (whatever that means).

At the time of the release of the

"translation" of *I Spit On Your Graves* , post-war France was welcoming the new American Literature: Katherine-Anne Porter, Erskine Caldwell, Horace MacCoy, Carson McCullers, and Richard Wright — the latter moved permanently to France in 1946. On the thriller-detective side, Marcel Duhamel had just created the famous "Série Noire" collection with Gallimard — still going strongly — which would make possible the diffusion of such authors as Raymond Chandler, Don Tracy, Raymond Marshall, and James Cain, not to mention British writers such as James Hadley Chase and Peter Cheyney. *I Spit On Your Graves* fits right into this racy literary climate, being overloaded with all the ingredients of the genre: racism (hate, intolerance, discrimination); sex (seduction, sexual athletics, rape); death (lynching, sadism, gore). Not a love story! And obviously, it was presented to the French reader as a "U.S. product."

Now we can begin to appreciate all the intricate levels of this violent thriller.

Vian, a white French man, writes (in French) a thriller staged in the USA (where he has actually never been). The hero is black, but looks white, and sets out to wreak vengeance against white society for the harm it has done to his brother. But he is bound to die, since his quest is a solitary one, and no hope exists for a just legal system or a just society. To legitimize its realistic subtext, Vian writes under the alleged signature of an African-American: Vernon Sullivan, while presenting himself as the translator (i.e. mediator). Despite the aspect of hoax here, which should not be overlooked in the case of Vian (who has used many pseudonyms), Boris Vian is dead serious about what he writes, and the way he writes it. He means all of it. True, he will later claim that this novel "hardly deserves attention, from a literary viewpoint" (in his afterword to Sullivan's second novel), but he also claims, at the same time, that, whether people speak well about it or not, they do speak about it, and that in itself makes the book a literary success.

For about a year and a half after its publication, people remained duped as to the authenticity of Sullivan. Then Vian rewrote his thriller, but this time in English (this present version), with the help of an American friend, Milton Rosenthal. He did this to validate the existence of the supposed original text behind his translation, let alone the unusual style of the English text. This English version, *I Spit On Your Graves* , was published in April 1948, the third novel by Sullivan, "translated" by Vian, was published, and by then the secret was out. The reading public had come to know that Sullivan and Vian were one and the same.

Who was this Boris Vian, who perpetrated this strange, multi-layer literary trick?

Boris Paul Vian was born on March 10, 1920, at Ville-d'Avray, near Paris. His family was middle-class, and until 1929 lived comfortably on private investments. In 1932 the young Boris manifested the first signs of a rheumatic heart. His interest in jazz started in the mid-thirties. At school, he was brilliant and very quick. In 1939, when the war broke out, he entered "École Centrale", the most prestigious French engineering school. He graduated in 1942. In 1941, he married Michelle Léglise. They had two children, Patrick and Carole. During the war years, he started writing poetry and short texts. From 1945 to 1950, he lived a very intense life. He wrote novels, short stories, poems, plays, pamphlets, jazz-chronicles, and did many translations.

Ironically, it was through his false translation of *I Spit On Your Graves* that he secured his first actual translation contract, for Kenneth Fearing's "The Big Clock."

During that time, he also played his trumpet frequently, at jam sessions and concerts (against medical advice). In 1950, he was tried (and heavily fined) for affront to public decency, as a result of his first two novels written under the Sullivan pseudonym. (This, as a result of the charges launched by Daniel Parker). From 1950 on, he entered a second phase in his life. He separated from and then divorced Michelle, stopped writing novels, and devoted his talents to songs, opera and sketches. In 1954 he married his second wife, Ursula Kubler, whom he had met in 1950.

The ill-fated *I Spit On Your Graves* eventually came back to haunt him. In 1959, a film adaptation was made, which he utterly rejected. On June 23, 1959, while he was watching the first frames of the cursed film, his heart stopped beating. He was pronounced dead a short while after. The rumor has it that his last words were, as he was commenting on the beginning of the film: "These guys are supposed to be American? my ass!"... So died Boris Vian, in a fit of anger, at the age of thirty-nine.

When he wrote *J'irai cracher sur vos tombes* , he had already written two long tales, two novels, and over one hundred sonnets, but nothing was yet published. We may assume then, that, while he was infusing his true sentiments regarding blatant racism against Blacks in the United States into his own literary production, and given his eagerness to be published, he did want to shake the coconut-tree. This is what he wrote in one of his numerous jazz-chronicles that he published weekly in Jazz-Hot No. 22, April 1948, my translation.

Today, as a result of the initiative of TamTam Books, the false translation signed by one of the most brilliant writers of post-war France is at last accessible to the American public. And it only took fifty years!

Marc Lapprand

Boris Vian

PREFACE

It was in July 1946 that Jean d'Halluin
met Sullivan at a sort of Franco-American
meeting. Two days later, Sullivan showed him
his manuscript.
In the meantime, he told him that he
considered himself more as a nigger than a
white man, in spite of having passed the "line";
we know that every year, several thousand
Negroes (thus designated by law), disappear
from the census lists and pass to the opposite
camp. His preference for Negroes inspired
Sullivan with a sort of contempt for "good nigger", those that the white people tapped affec-
tionately on the back in literature. He had the
idea that one can imagine and also meet
Negroes just as "tough" as white men. This is
what he had personally tried to demonstrate in
this short novel of which Jean d'Halluin
acquired the complete publication rights as
soon as he heard about it through a friend.
Sullivan did not hesitate about leaving his
manuscript in France, all the more so as his
American publishers had just shown him the
timidity of any attempt to publication in his
country.
Here, our well-known moralists will

reproach certain pages their... realism a little advanced. It seems to us interesting to emphasize the main difference existing between these and the stories of Miller; this latter does not hesitate, in any case, to use the most vivid vocabulary; on the contrary it seems that Sullivan thinks more of suggesting by a turn of expression and construction of a sentence than by the crude word. In this respect, he comes nearer to a more Latin erotic tradition.

 We meet, besides, in these pages, the extremely clear influence of Cain (in spite of the fact that the author does not seek to justify, by an artifice, written or otherwise, the use of the first person, of which the writer mentioned proclaims the necessity in the curious preface of "Three of a kind", a collection of three short stories recently assembled in America in one book and translated here by Sabine Beritz); and one by the equally ultra-modern Chase and other supporters of what is shocking. In this respect we must acknowledge that Sullivan shows himself really much more of a sadist than his illustrious predecessors; it is not surprising that his book should have been refused in America : we wager it would be banned the day following its publication. As for its back-ground, one must see a manifestation of a desire for revenge in a race still, what

ever one may say, over-worked, badly treated,
and terrorized, a sort of temptation of exor-
cism, against the domination of "real whites",
in the same manner that paleolithic men paint-
ed bisons transperced with arrows to allure
their prey to the traps, a quite considerable
contempt for the probability and also the con-
cessions of the public tastes.

Alas, America, land of cockayne,
is also the chosen land of puritans, of drunk-
ards, and of those people who say "bear that
well in mind"; and if in France, we strive to
more originality, on the other side of the
Atlantic, no anxiety is felt in exploiting
unblushingly a formula which has proved its
value. In all sincerity it is as good a way as
any other of selling one's writings....

Boris Vian

I

Nobody knew me at Buckton. That's why Clem picked the place; besides, even if I hadn't had a flat, I didn't have enough gas to go any farther north. Just about a gallon. I had a dollar, and Clem's letter, and that's all. There wasn't a thing worth a damn in my valise, so let's not mention it. Hold on: I did have in the bag the kid's little revolver, a miserable, cheap little .22 caliber pea-shooter. It was still in his pocket when the sheriff came to tell us to take the body away to bury it. I've got to say that I counted on Clem's letter more than on everything else. It ought to work, it just had to work. I looked at my hands on the steering wheel, at my fingers, my nails. Nobody would find anything wrong there. No risk on that score. Maybe I'd get away with it.

My brother Tom had known Clem at the University. Clem never treated him like he did the other students. He was glad to talk to him. They drank together, went out together in Clem's Cadillac. It was because of Clem that people put up with Tom. When he left to take his father's place at the head of his factory, Tom had to decide to leave too. He came back to us. He'd learned a lot and didn't have much trouble getting an appointment as a teacher in the new school. And then the business with the kid ruined everything. I could have been a hypocrite and kept my mouth shut, but not the kid. He didn't see anything wrong in it. So the girl's father and brother took care of him.

That's why my brother gave me the letter to Clem. I couldn't stay in that town any longer and he wrote to Clem to find me something.

Not too far away, so he could see me once in a while, but far enough so nobody would know me. He thought that with my face and my personality I wouldn't get into trouble. Maybe he was right, but I still couldn't forget the kid. Buckton Bookstore manager - that was my new job. I was to get into touch with the present manager and learn the job in three days. He was getting a new managership, a better one, and wanted to make a name for himself.

It was nice and sunny. The street's name had been changed to Pearl Harbor Street. Clem probably didn't know it. You could still see the old name on the signs. The store's number was 270. I stopped the Nash right in front of the door. The manager was sitting behind the register, copying some numbers into an account-book. He was about 40 years old, with hard blue eyes and light blond hair, as I noticed when I opened the door. I said hello.

"How do you do! Can I help you?"

"Yes, this letter is for you."

"Oh, so you're the one I'm supposed to break in here. Let's see the letter."

He took it, read it, turned it over, and gave it back to me.

"It isn't very complicated," he said. "There's the stock (he made a sweeping motion with his arm). The accounts will be straight tonight. As far as selling and advertising and everything else, follow the suggestions of the inspectors from the main office and the circulars you'll get."

"This is a chain-outlet?"

"Yes."

"O.K." I said, "What do you sell most of?"

"Oh, novels. Bad novels, but that isn't our affair. Religious books, pretty fair, and text-books too. Not many children's books, nor any serious stuff either. I never tried to build up that line."

"You mean that in your opinion religious books aren't serious?"

He licked his lips.

"Don't be saying I said something which I didn't say."

I laughed heartily

"No need to get mad, that's what I think too."

"In that case, let me give some advice. Don't let anybody else know it, and go to church every Sunday, cause otherwise you're not going to have many customers."

"Oh alright," I said, "so I'll go to church."

"Here," he said, handing me a sheet of paper, "Check that. It's the accounting for last month. It's pretty simple. You get all your books from the main office. All you've got to do is keep a record, in triplicate, of what you get and what you sell. They come to collect twice a month. You get paid by check, a commission on sales."

"Let me see it," I said.

I took the form and sat down on a low counter, cluttered up with books the customers had taken off the shelves and had been too rushed to put back.

"What's there for a guy to do in this town?" I asked him.

"Not a damn thing." There are the girls in the drug-store across the street, and you can get some Bourbon in Ricardo's, couple of blocks up the street."

I found him pleasant, with his brusque way of talking.

"How long have you been living here?"

"Five years," he said. "Still got five to go."

"And then?"

"You're too damn nosy."

"Don't blame me. Why'd you say you've got five more to go. I didn't ask you."

His mouth became less harsh, and he crinkled his eyes.

"I guess you're right. O.K., then-five more years and I quit."

"What are you going to do?"

"Write," he said. "Write best-sellers. Nothing but best-sellers. Historical novels; novels where colored men sleep with white women and don't get lynched; novels about pure young girls who manage to grow up unblemished by the vicious small-town life which surrounds them."

He chuckled.

"Yep, best-sellers. And then some very daring and original novels. It doesn't require much to be daring in this part of the world. All you've got to do is write about things everybody knows, and take a little trouble in doing it."

"You'll get there," I said.

"Sure I'll get there. I've got six of 'em ready right now."

"Never tried to get them published?"

"I'm not pals with any publisher, and I haven't got enough dough to pay for them myself."

"So what are you going to do?"

"Well in five years I'll have the money."

"I guess you'll make it," I told him.

There was plenty of work from then on, in spite of the store's uncomplicated administrative arrangements. I had to bring the order lists up to date, and then Hansen, as the former manager was called, gave me all sorts of tips about the customers, a certain number of whom came regularly to see him and talk about books. About all they knew about literature they learned from the "Saturday Review" or from the book reviews of the paper published in the State capital, which had a circulation of about sixty thousand. For the time being I did no more than listen to them talk with Hansen, trying to remember their names and their faces, since in a bookstore, more than anywhere else, its damn important to greet the customer with "Good Morning, Mr. Soandso" as soon as he comes in the door.

Hansen fixed me up with a place to live

too. I took over the two rooms which he had been renting just above the drugstore across the street. He'd loaned me a couple of dollars, enough to stay at the hotel for three days, and he was considerate enough to invite me to eat with him an average of twice a day, thus keeping me from running up a big monetary debt with him, since I had no one else to borrow from. He was a nice guy. I was somewhat concerned about this plan of his to write best-sellers : you don't write best-sellers just like that, even if you do have dough. Maybe he did have talent. For his sake, I hoped so.

On the third day, he took me to Ricardo's to have a drink before lunch. It was ten o'clock, and he was leaving in the afternoon.

It was the last meal we were going to have together. After that I would have to handle the customers by myself, and the town too. I had to make good. Running into Hansen had been a stroke of luck. With my luck I might have lived a couple of days, peddling something or other, but this way I was getting off to a good start.

Ricardo's was the usual bar and grill, somewhat clean, thoroughly ugly. There was a funny combination of smells about the place, like doughnuts fried in onions, if that were possible. A character behind the bar was absorbed in a newspaper.

"What'll you have?" he asked, automatically.

"A couple of Bourbons," Hansen ordered, looking at me questioningly.

I nodded.

The barkeep gave us two big glasses with ice and straws.

"I always take it like that," Hansen apologized. "Don't drink it if you don't want to."

"Try anything once," I said.

If you've never drunk iced Bourbon with a straw, you can't imagine what an effect it has. Like a stream of fire on your palate. Sweet fire, something terrible.

"Good stuff!" I gasped.

I caught a glimpse of myself in the mirror. I looked rather dazed. I hadn't been doing much drinking lately. Hansen broke into a laugh.

"Don't let it get you down. It won't take you long to get used to it, unfortunately I guess. As for me," he continued, "I guess I'll have to break in the bartender at the next bar I do my drinking at."

"I'm sorry you're leaving," I said.

I Spit on Your Graves

He laughed.

"If I stayed, you would have to leave. I
think it's better that I go. More than five years
- Christ, that's a long time."

He finished his drink with one long sip,
and ordered another.

"You'll manage, alright." He looked me
up and down. "You're O.K. There's something
about you I can't put my finger on. Your
voice."

I just smiled. He was too damn discern-
ing.

"Your voice is too full. You don't happen to be a singer?"

"Oh, I sing sometimes, just for fun."

I hadn't been doing any more singing. I
did before, before the business with the kid. I
would sing to my own accompaniment on the
guitar. I could sing some blues, and some old
New Orleans songs, and some melodies I
made up myself for the guitar, but I didn't feel
like playing any more. What I needed was
money. Lots of it. To carry out my plans.

"The women will all fall for you
with that voice of yours," Hansen said.

I shrugged.

"Not interested?"

He gave me a hearty slap on the back.

"Just stroll over towards the drugstore.

You'll find them all there. They've got a club in this town. The bobby-soxers' club. You know the girls, - every last one of them with their flashy sox and sloppy sweaters. And they all write fan letters to Frank Sinatra. The drugstore is their hangout. You must have noticed. No, I guess not, you've kept yourself cooped up in the store every day."

I took another Bourbon for myself. It went down into my arms, my legs, my whole body.

Down there, we didn't have any bobby-soxers. I wouldn't have minded. Girls of fifteen, with little pointed breasts under their tight sweaters - they do it on purpose, the little witches. And their socks, bright yellow and red and green sox, sticking up out of their flat-heeled shoes. And flair skirts, and round knees. And always sitting on the ground with their legs spread so you could see their flesh undies. Yes, I liked their looks, the bobby-soxers.

Hansen was looking at me.

"They all will," he said. "You don't have to worry about a thing. They know lots of places to take you to."

"Don't be such a pig," I said.

"Oh, no," he said, "I meant places to take you dance and have a drink."

He smiled. It must have been all over my face that I was interested.

"They're funny,' he said. "They'll come to see you in the store."

"What would they want there?"

"Oh, they'll buy pictures of movie stars, and, quite by accident, of course, all the books on psychoanalysis. Medical books, I mean. They all seem to be studying medicine."

"Alright," I muttered, "We'll see."

And now I really had to appear indifferent, because Hansen turned to another subject. Then, when we had finished lunch, he went away about two in the afternoon. I was left alone in front of the store.

II

I must have been there about two
weeks when I began to feel bored. All that
time I hadn't left the store. The sales were
going fine. The advertising took care of everything in advance, and the books sold. Every
week the main office sent, together with the
books on consignment, a mass of illustrated
leaflets and throwaways, and display material
to be put in a good spot in the window, under
the book in question or in full view. Most of
the time, all I had to do was read the blurb on
the jacket, open the book at four or five different spots to get a good idea of its contents,
good enough, in any case, to give a spiel that
would take in the average customer especially
after the effect of the illustrated jacket, the
folders, the picture of the author with the short
biographical sketch. It costs a lot to put out a
book, and all the dressing is for a good purpose - it shows clearly too that most people
don't care about getting good books : what
they really want is to have read the book rec-
ommended by their club, the book of the
moment, and they don't give a rap about the
contents.

I would get an enormous amount of

certain books, with a note recommending a window display, and quantities of throw-aways. I put a pile of them next to the cash-register and slipped one into every book sold. Nobody refuses a book-circular on shiny paper, and the few blurbs they carry are just the ticket for the sort of readers you find in this town. The main office used this system for all books of a somewhat sexy nature, and they were usually all gone a few hours after I displayed them.

To tell the truth, I wasn't really bored. But I was beginning to get the hang of the routine in the place, and I had time to think about other things. That's what bothered me. Things were going too well.

The weather was nice. It was river, toward the end of summer. The dust hung in the air over the town. Down along the it must have been cool under the trees. I hadn't been out once since I'd come, and I didn't know anything about the surrounding country-side. I felt that I needed a change of air. But one thing really bothered me. I wanted a woman.

That afternoon when I pulled over the collapsible iron-latticework at five o'clock, I didn't go back into the store to work as usual, under the fluorescent lights. I took my hat and, carrying my jacket on my arm, I went straight across the street to the drugstore. I had a room upstairs. There were three customers in the place, a boy of about fifteen and two girls of about the same age. They looked at me absently and turned back to their milk shakes. The very sight of the shakes gave me the shakes. Fortunately I had a good remedy for that right in my jacket-pocket.

I sat down at the counter, a seat away from the tallest of the two girls. The waitress, a homely looking brunette gave me a vague look.

"What have you got besides milk drinks?'

"Lemon and lime," she suggested, "Grapefruit juice, tomato juice, coke?"

"Grapefruit juice," I said, "and don't fill the glass up, either."

I felt in my jacket-pocket, and unscrewed the flask-cap.

"No liquor here," the waitress objected meekly.

"It's alright. It's my medicine," I gave a laugh. "Don't worry about your license."

I handed her a dollar. I had gotten my check that morning. Ninety bucks a week. Clem sure knew the right people. She gave me my change, and I left her a dime tip.

Grapefruit juice and bourbon isn't exactly a drink, but its better than nothing. I felt better, - I 'd snap out of it. I was snapping out of it. The three kids were looking at me. For kids like that at twenty-six I was an old man. I smiled at the little blond. She had on a sky-blue sweater with white stripes, no collar, the sleeves pushed up above the elbow, and little white sox in thick crepe-soled shoes. She was cute. Nice breasts. Probably firm to the touch, like ripe plums. She didn't have a brassiere on and the nipples stuck out through the fabric. She smiled back at me.

"Hot, isn't it?" I said to break the ice.

"Awful," she said, stretching herself.

There were sweat-stains under her armpits. That did something to me. I got up and slipped a nickel into the slot of the juke-box near the window.

"Feel like dancing?" I said, coming over to her.

"It'll probably kill me," she said.

She pressed up against me so hard I lost my breath. She smelled like a fresh-ly washed baby. She was slender, and I could reach her right shoulder with my right hand. I reached out with my arm, and slid my fingers in just under her breast. The others had been watching us, and they danced too. It was the hit-song "Shoo Fly Pie" with vocal by Dinah Shore. The girl hummed the melody as she danced. The waitress had lifted her nose out of her magazine when we started dancing, but turned back to it after a minute or so.

She didn't have a thing on under her sweater. I could feel it right away. I was glad when the record ended. Another two minutes and I wouldn't have been able to control myself any more. She let me go, went back to her seat, and looked at me.

"You don't dance at all bad for some-body as old as you are."

"It was my grandpop who taught me," I said.

"You can tell that easy," she returned the kidding, "Not the least bit hep."

"You won't find me so handy with your jive, but I bet there's plenty of other tricks I could teach you."

She dropped her eyelashes and looked at me through half closed eyes.

"Grown up tricks?"

"That depends on you."

"I can guess what you're leading up to..." she said.

"I'm not so sure you do. Do any of you have a guitar?"

"You play the guitar?" said the boy.

He seemed to wake up all of a sudden.

"A little," I said.

"Then you sing too," the other girl said.

"A little."

"He's got a voice just like Cab Calloway's," the first one put in.

She seemed to be a little mad at seeing the others talk to me. I'd better take it easy.

"Take me somewhere where I can get my hands on a guitar and I'll show you what I can do. I don't claim to be the father of the blues himself, but I can play them."

She looked straight at me.

"O.K." she said, "we'll go to B.J.'s."

"He's got a guitar?"

"She's got a guitar, Betty Jane."

"It could have stood for Barney, Junior." I exclaimed.

"Yeah," she said. "She lives over here, come on!"

"Right away?' the boy said.

"Why not?" I said. "She's got to be convinced."

"O.K." the boy said, "My name is Dick. She's Jicky."

He pointed to the girl I'd danced with.

"I'm Judy," said the other girl.

"And I'm Lee Anderson," I said. "I run

the bookstore across the street."

"We know," said Jicky. "Everybody has
known it for the past two weeks.

"That interested?"

"Sure thing," said Judy. "We
could use some men in this town."

The four of us went out in spite of
Dick's objections. They looked rather excited.
I still had enough whiskey left to hop them up
a little more if necessary.

"I'm all yours" I said when we were outside.

Dick's roadster, an ancient Chrysler, was
parked at the curb. He took the two girls up
front with him, and I made myself comfortable
in the back.

"How do you kids keep yourselves
busy," I asked.

The car took off smoothly, and Jicky got
on her knees on the front seat, turned toward
me.

"We work," she said.

"Schoolwork?" I suggested.

"That and other things."

"If you come back here," I said, raising
my voice a little because of the wind, "it'd be
easier to talk."

"Maybe," she murmured.

She again lowered her eyelids.

She must have picked up the trick in some movie.

"Afraid to get in a bad spot?"

"No-o" she said.

I grabbed her by the shoulders and swung her over the seat.

"Hey you," said Judy, turning around, "that's a funny way of talking."

I was shifting Jicky over to my left, and was maneuvering to grab her in the right spots. She sure was something to grab hold of. She seemed to know what was cooking. I put her down on the leather seat, and put my arm around her neck.

"Quiet now," I said, "Or I'll give you a spanking."

"What have you got in that bottle?" she asked.

I had my jacket on my knees. She slid her hand in and, I don't know whether she did it on purpose or not, but she hit the right spot.

"Hold tight," I said, drawing out her hand. "I'll give you some."

I screwed the metal cap off and offered her the flask. She took a good slug.

"Leave some for us," hollered Dick.

He was looking at us in the rear-view mirror.

"Be a fellow and let me have some, Lee".

"Don't worry, there's plenty more."

He steered with one hand, and stretched out the other towards us.

"Take it easy, won't you," Judy objected. "Don't land us in a ditch."

"Don't be a wet blanket. Don't you ever let yourself go?"

"Never!" she said defiantly.

She snatched the flask out of Dick's hands as he was about to give it back to me. When I got it, it was empty.

"Well!" I said approvingly, "feel better now?"

"Oh! its not so bad," she said.

I could see the tears showing in her eyes, but she held up alright. Her voiced sounded a bit choked.

"Damn, said Jicky, "there's no more left for me."

"We'll go after some more," I suggested.

Let's get the guitar first and then we'll go back to Ricardo's."

"You're lucky," the boy said. "Nobody'll sell us any."

"That's what you get for looking so young," I kidded them.

"Not as young as that," Jicky said angrily.

She squirmed about and got into such a

position that all I had to do was press with my
fingers to keep me well occupied. The roadster suddenly stopped, and I dropped my
hand on her arm.

"Be right back," Dick cried.

He got out and ran to the house. It was
one of a whole row, obviously built by the
same company on contract. Dick reappeared
on the porch. He had a guitar in a shiny case.
Slamming the door behind him, he was back
in the car in a couple of jumps.

"B.J. isn't here," he told us. "What're we
going to do?"

"We'll bring it back to her," I said,
"Climb in. Drive to Ricardo's and I'll get this
baby filled up."

"You're going to get yourself a nice reputation," said Judy.

"I'm not worried," I assured her.
"Everybody'll understand right away that
you're the ones who dragged me into your
wild orgies."

We turned around, but now the guitar
was in my way. I told the boy to stop a short
ways before the bar, and I got out to get a refill.
I bought an extra flask, and went back to the
bunch. Dick and Judy, on their knees on the
front seat, were in a hot argument with the
blond.

"What do you say, Lee", said the boy, "How about going swimming?"

"O.K." I said, "Got a pair of trunks to loan me? I haven't got a thing here."

"Oh, we'll manage," he said.

He took off, and we drove out of town. Almost immediately he took a little side road, just wide enough for the Chrysler and in pretty bad shape. In no shape at all, as a matter of fact.

"We've got a swell spot to go swimming," he said. "Nobody ever goes there. Swell water, too."

"Trout stream?"

"Yep. Gravel and white sand. Never see a soul there. We're the only ones that ever take this road."

"You can see that," I said, holding my jaw which I was afraid might get jolted off at the next bump. "You should trade this baby in for a half-track or something."

"It's all part of the fun," he explained. "It keeps people from sticking their dirty noses into our spot."

He stepped on the gas, and I offered up my soul to my maker. The road took a sudden turn and after another five hundred feet it just gave out. There were just some thick bushes there. The Chrysler stopped just before a big maple and Dick and Judy jumped out. I then got out and lifted Jicky out. Dick had taken the guitar and led the way. I picked my way after him. There was a narrow path under the branches and we suddenly came on the stream, clear and cool as a glass of gin. The sun was pretty low in the sky, but it was still very hot. On one side the water rippled in the shade and on the other it glistened brightly in the slanting rays of the sun. A patch of thick, dry, almost powdery grass went right down to the stream.

"This spot isn't bad at all," I said approvingly. "D'ya find it all by yourselves?"

"Do you take us for some little dopes," said Jicky.

And a clod of dry earth hit me on the neck.

"If you don't behave right, I won't give you any more milk", and I patted my pocket to make sure they understood.

"Oh, don't get mad, nice old blues-singer," she said. "How about showing us what you can do."

"How about the trunks?" I asked Dick.

"You won't need any," he said. "Nobody ever comes here."

I turned around. Judy had already

taken off her sweatshirt. She sure wasn't wearing much under it. Her skirt slipped down her legs, and in a jiffy, she kicked off her socks and shoes. She stretched out on the grass, completely nude. I must have had a dopey expression on my face, since she laughed at me in such a mocking manner that I almost forgot myself. Dick and Jicky, now dressed in the same uniform, lay down beside her. As a result of their laughter, I was the one who felt embarrassed. I nevertheless took notice that the boy was very skinny, his ribs sticking out under his sun-tanned skin.

"O.K.." I said, "I'm game."

I purposely took my time. I appreciated what a fine body I had, and I made sure that they had the time to appreciate it too while I was undress-
ing. I gave myself a good stretch, crackling my bones, and then I sat down next
to them. I still wasn't completely calmed down from my campaign with Jicky, but I didn't try to hide anything. I suppose they had expected me to go down.

I grabbed the guitar. It was an excellent Ediphone. I didn't like to play sitting on the ground so I said to Dick.

"O.K. with you if I go after the car-seat?"

"I'll go with you," Jicky said.

She slithered through the bushes like an eel. It was a funny effect she made with her boyish body and her face like a Hollywood starlet, in the middle of the bushes with their dark shadows. I put down the guitar and followed her. She had a good start on me, and by the time I reached the car, she was coming back, carrying the heavy leather seat.

"Let me have it," I said.

"Let me alone, Tarzan!" she cried.

I paid no attention to her protestations, and I grabbed her roughly by the behind. She dropped the seat and didn't object. I was hot enough to have jumped a monkey. She must have realized it, for she gave me a tough tussle. I broke out into a happy laugh. I liked that. The grass was high in that spot, and soft as a rubber mattress. She slipped onto the ground and I went down too. We wrestled about like a couple of savages. She was tanned to the tips of her breasts, and didn't have the brassiere-marks that disfigure so many nude women. As smooth as silk, and naked as a babe, but when I finally got her under me, I learned right quick that she was no baby. She gave me the best sample of technique I'd had in many a moon. My fingers felt the hollows and curves of her back, and farther down, her buttocks, hard as a watermel-

on. We kept it up for about ten minutes. She
made out as though she were sleeping, and
just as I was going all the way, she dropped me
like a hot potato and ran away from me
towards the river. I picked up the seat and ran
after her. At the edge of the stream she sprint-
ed and dove into the water without a splash.

"You're going in already?"

It was Judy's voice. She was chewing
on a blade of grass, stretched out on her back,
her hands under her head. Dick, sprawled out
beside her, was caressing her thighs. One of
the two flasks was tossed aside on the ground.
She caught my look.

"Yep, it's empty." she giggled. "We left
you one".

Jicky paddled about on the other side of
the stream. I felt around in my jacket and took
out the other bottle, and then dived in. The
water was warm. I felt I was in perfect form. I
swam with a heavy stroke and reached her out
in the middle of the stream. It was just over
our heads and there was hardly any current.

"Thirsty?" I asked her, moving one arm
about to keep me up.

"Are you kidding," she replied. "You'll
just kill me with your drug-store cowboy manners."

"Come on," I said, "Try to float."

She turned over on her back, and
I slipped in under her, one arm around her
middle. I gave her the flask with my other
hand. She took it, and I let my fingers stroke
her thighs. I slowly spread her legs and I
again took her there in the stream. She let herself go onto me. We turned almost vertical,
moving just enough to keep off the bottom.

III

It went on like that until September. There were five or six other kids in their bunch, boys and girls: B.J., who owned the guitar, a girl with a funny figure but whose skin gave off a most remarkable perfume. Susie Ann, another blond, more shapely than Jicky; and a girl with chestnut hair, 100% scatterbrained who danced all day long. The boys were as dumb as I could hope for. I hadn't repeated the mistake of leaving town in their company. It wouldn't have taken long and I would have been in trouble. We met now at the stream, and they kept the secret because I was an easy source of whiskey and gin for them.

I had all the girls, one after the other, but it was a bit too easy, it almost turned my stomach. They did it as easily and regularly as though they'd been taught it in school hygiene, like brushing their teeth. They acted like a bunch of monkeys, untidy, greedy, chattering, vicious. I kept myself busy with them for the time being. I often played the guitar for them; that alone would have been enough, even if I hadn't been able to spank them all together with one hand tied behind my back. They taught me to jitterbug and to talk jive : it didn't

take me long to do it better than they. Nothing
they could do about it either.

I still couldn't get the kid off my mind
and I wasn't sleeping well. I'd seen Tom a couple of times. He managed to get along. We
never talked about the business down there
any more. They didn't bother Tom in his
school, and as for me, they hadn't ever seen me
much. Anne Moran's father had sent her to
the State University. He kept things going
with his son. Tom asked me if everything was
alright with me, and I told him that my bank
account had already reached a hundred and
twenty dollars. I was stingy with everything
but liquor, and the book sales were still excellent. I hoped for a raise towards the end of the
summer. He counseled me not to neglect my
religious devotions That was one thing I'd
been able to free myself of in my mind, but I
made sure that other people didn't notice it.
Tom believed in God. I just went to church
every Sunday like Hansen, but I think you
can't keep a clear head and believe in God
both, and I had to keep a clear head.

After church, we'd meet at the stream
and take the girls in turn, with the same
degree of modesty as a holy menagerie of
monkeys in rut. That's just about what we
were, you can take it from me. And then the

summer went by without our even knowing it, and it began to rain.

I often went back to Ricardo's. Occasionally I went to the drugstore to cut a rug with the cats that hung out in the joint. As I said, I was able to talk their jive better than they-maybe it was in my blood. A whole crowd of the richer bunch in Buckton began to come back from their vacations at the seashore or in the mountains and Lord knows where. Skins well tanned, hair bleached, but no more than ours, that is of those who'd spent the summer at the stream. The store became one of their favorite rendez-vous.

They still didn't know me, that bunch, but I had plenty of time and I didn't rush things.

IV

And then Dexter came back too. They had all been talking about him enough to drive me batty. He lived in one of the swankest houses in the nice part of town. His parents stayed in New York, but he spent most of the year in Buckton, because of his delicate health. They originally came from Buckton, and it was as good a place to study as any. I already knew all about his Packard, his golf-clubs, his radio console, his bar and his liquor stock as though I'd spent my whole life in his place : When I finally saw him I wasn't disappointed. He was exactly the miserable little bastard that he should have been. A skinny guy, dark, almost Indian-like with black, shifty eyes, a thin mouth under a big hooked nose, yet with curly hair. He had horrible looking hands, big paws with short broad nails, wider than they were long and giving the effect of running crosswise across his fingers. They were swollen too and made you think of something unhealthy.

They were all after Dexter like some mutts scrapping over a bit of meat. I lost some of my importance as a source of liquor, but I

still had the guitar and I had also saved up
some specialties they had no previous notion
of. I had plenty of time. I was waiting for
worthwhile game and I was sure that in
Dexter's bunch I would find just what I had
been hoping for ever since I'd been dreaming
about the kid every night. I think Dexter liked
me, after a fashion. He must have hated me
because of my muscles and my body, and also
because of my guitar, but I guess it attracted
him too. I had everything he didn't have. And
he had plenty of dough. We'd make a good
pair. And besides, he'd understood from the
very beginning that I was willing to try at-I'm
sure he didn't go that far-how could he have
suspected it any better than the others.
He just figured, I think, that together with me
he could organize some real wild orgies. A far
as that goes, he wasn't wrong.

  The town's population had now come
back to normal; I was beginning to sell school
books such as general science, physics, geolo-
gy, and stuff like that. They sent all their
school friends to me. The girls were pretty
bad. At the age of fourteen their main interest
had already become to get themselves petted,
and you've really got to try hard to find a pre-
text for that in buying a book. But they always

managed : they made me feel their biceps so I
could see how they'd built them up during
their vacations, and then, bit by bit, they got
me down to their thighs. They overdid it.
After all, I had some serious customers and I
had to look out for my job. But these kids at
any time of the day were as hot as a bitch in
heat, and must have had wet panties all the
time. I don't think being a college teacher can
be a very restful job, if an ordinary bookseller
can go so far so easy. When school started
again, I was a lot better off. Then they came
only in the afternoon. What's worse is that the
boys liked me too. They were neither male nor
female, most of them except for some that
were already built like men, most of them got
as much pleasure as the girls from having me
feel them. And then there was their damn
dancing anywhere any time. I don't remember
ever having seen five of them together without
their beginning to hum some popular hit and
then start hopping. In a way that made me feel
good for I knew that came from my people.

I didn't worry any more about my being
caught. I think I showed nothing suspicious.
Dexter had frightened me one of the last times
we went swimming. I was clowning with one
of the girls, no clothes on of course, tossing her
into the air and rolling her on my arms like a

little baby. He was watching us, stretched out on his belly behind me. He was an ugly sight with his sickly body and the scars on his back from the drainages when he'd had his twice repeated onsets of pleurisy.

He looked up at me and said:

"You know you're not built like everybody else, Lee, you've got the same kind of drooping shoulders as a colored prizefighter."

I dropped the girl and tensed into alertness, and I danced about him singing some lyrics I'd made up, and everybody laughed, but I didn't feel good. Dexter didn't laugh. He just looked at me.

That night, when I looked in the mirror over my washstand, it was my turn to laugh. There wasn't a thing I had to worry about with the blond hair I saw there, the pink and white skin. I'd take them all in. It was jealousy that had made Dexter talk that way. And then, I really did have drooping shoulders. So what? I hardly ever slept as well as I did that night. A couple of days later, they organized a party at Dexter's house for the weekend. Evening dress. I rented a tux which it didn't take the tailor long to fit to me. They guy who'd worn it before me must have had just about my build, and it wasn't bad at all.

That night too, I thought of the kid.

V

As soon as I was in Dexter's house, I understood why they'd specified evening dress : our bunch was lost in a majority of "better class" people. I recognized some of them at once : the doctor, the preacher and others of the same type. A colored servant took my hat, and I noticed a couple of others. Then Dexter took me by the arm to introduce me to his parents. I learned that it was his birthday. His mother looked like him : a little, skinny, dark-haired woman, with muddy eyes, and his father was the sort of man you feel like smothering slowly with a pillow, they have such a superior air about them. B.J., Judy, Jicky and the others, all dressed up in evening dresses, were acting very properly. I couldn't keep from thinking of their boxes when I saw them ceremoniously drink their cocktails and accept the invitations of some serious looking characters in cheaters who asked them to dance. From time to time we gave each other a wink to keep our spirits up. It was pretty miserable.

They really had the liquor though. Dexter did know how to treat his pals. I asked a couple of girls to dance a rumba without being properly introduced, and I drank-that's about all there was to do. A good number with Judy picked me up again-she was one of the girls I hardly ever laid. She usually seemed to avoid me and I never went after her more than after any other, but that evening I thought I'd never get out from between her legs-boy, was she hot! She wanted me to go up to Dexter's room, but I wasn't sure we wouldn't be bothered there so I took her to have a drink instead, and then, I saw a group of four people come in and I felt as though I'd been jolted by a mule.

There were three women - two of them young and the other about forty, and a man - but who cares about them. I felt that I'd at last found what I wanted. Those two young ones, and the kid would squirm in his grave with joy. I grabbed Judy's arm - she must have thought I was going to take her, for she snuggled up against me. I would have liked to stretch them all out in my bed together, just to look at them. I let Judy go and stroked her buttocks casually as I dropped my arm.

"Who are those two dolls, Judy?"

"Interested, aren't you, you vicious old postcard peddler?"

"Where did Dexter ever dig up those two knock-outs?"

"High society. No small town bobby-soxers there, Lee. Not the type we could take swimming with us."

"A damn shame too. As a last resort I think I'd even take on the old one as long as I could have the young ones too."

"Don't be getting so hot and bothered, cutypie. They're not local girls."

"Where do they come from?"

"Prixville. About a hundred miles away. Old friends of Dexter's old man."

"Both of them?"

"What do you think! You're pretty slow tonight, punchy. They're sisters, with their father and mother. Lou and Jean Asquith. Jean is the blond. The older one. Lou is five years younger."

"That makes her sixteen?" I hazarded.

"Fifteen. Lee Anderson, are you going to ditch our bunch and chase after papa Asquith's fillies?"

"Don't be a drip, Judy. Don't they appeal to you?"

"No thank you, I feel pretty normal tonight. I prefer men. Let's dance, Lee."

"Will you introduce me?"

"Ask Dexter."

"O.K." I said.

We danced the last two bars of the record that was just finishing, and I left her. Dexter was giving a line to some skirt at the other end of the hall. I latched on to him.

"Say, Dexter!"

"Yeah!"

He turned around. He had a mocking air as he looked at me, but I didn't give a rap.

"Those girls over there, the Asquiths I think. Give me a knockdown."

"Sure thing, old man, come on."

They appeared even more stunning close-up than when I'd seen them from the bar. They were sensational. I made some insignificant remark to them and then invited Lou, the dark-haired one, to dance the dreamy number the record changer had just put on. Glory! I blessed the Lord and the guy who had had a tux made in my size. I held her a bit closer than proper, but nevertheless I couldn't press her up against me like we in the bunch did, when we felt like it. She had used a rather subtle perfume, which must have been very expensive; probably really from Paris. Her dark hair was heaped up on one side of the head, and her yellowish lynx-eyes shone out of a rather pale V-shaped face. And her body - rather not think about it. Her dress seemed to hold up by itself, I don't know just how, since there was nothing over her shoulders or around her neck, noting but her breasts to hold it up, and I must say that they looked so hard and pointy that they would have held up a couple of dozen dresses of that weight. I shifted her a bit to the right and I could feel the point through my dress shirt, on my chest. You could see the others' underwear pressing up under their dresses, but she had fixed herself up differently, for from her armpits down to her ankles her form was as smooth as though poured into a mold. After I had gotten my breath back, I dared to try to talk to her.

"How is it that I've never seen you here before?"

"But I do come here, as you can see."

She drew back a bit so she could look at me. I was at least a head taller than she.

"I mean, here in town."

"You'd see me if you came to Prixville."

"Then I think I'll have to make my home in Prixville."

I had hesitated before speaking so bluntly. I didn't want to go too fast, but you could never tell with women. You've got to take a chance. It didn't seem to bother her. She smiled a little, but her eyes were still cold.

"Even then you wouldn't necessarily see

me."

"I suppose all your admirers keep you hidden."

I was certainly going at it too crudely. I don't usually do that when I'm not excited.

"Oh," she said, "There aren't too many interesting people in Prixville."

"Well that's fine," I said, "Then I still have a chance!"

"I don't know that you're at all interesting."

Well, I'd asked for it and she gave it to me. But I wasn't going to give up that easy.

"Just what do you find interesting?"

"Well, you're not so bad. But you never can tell. I don't know you."

"I'm a friend of Dexter's, of Dick Page and the others."

"I know Dick. But Dexter is a funny sort of fellow."

"He's got too much money for you to call him that," I said.

"In that case I guess you won't be thinking much of my family either. You know, we're not too gad off as far as money goes either."

"You can sense that," I said, dropping my head to sniff her hair.

She smiled again.

"You like my perfume?"

"Love it!"

"That's funny," she said. "I could have sworn you'd prefer the smell of horses, of gun grease, or of witch hazel."

"Don't be making fun of me," I said. "It isn't my fault if I'm built the way I am and that I don't look like a little angel."

"I hate little angels," she said. "But I dislike even more men that like horses."

"I never want to get within a mile of the critters," I said. "When can I see you again."

"Oh! I haven't left yet. You've still got the whole evening."

"That isn't enough."

"That'll depend on you."

At this point the number finished, and she just left me. I watched her slip through the other couples, and she turned around to laugh at me, but it wasn't a very discouraging laugh. She had a figure that would have awakened even a Congressman.

I went back to the bar. I found Dick and Jicky there. They were sipping some Martinis. They seemed to be bored stiff.

"Hey, Dick," I said to him, "Don't laugh so hard, you're liable to get your neck out of joint."

"What's cooking with you, long hair?"

said Jicky. "What've you been up to. Shagging with a nigger-woman. Or chasing the chicken with the golden egg."

"For a longhair," I snapped back, "I can be pretty groovy. Let's get some solid cats rounded up and make tracks to where I can show you who's a square.

"You mean nice little cats with lynx-eyes and strapless gowns, huh?"

"Jicky, sugar-baby," I said going over to her and grabbing her by the wrists, "you don't blame me for going for good-looking females, do you?"

I pulled her up against me and looked into her eyes. She gave me a broad smile.

"You're getting tired of us, Lee. Got enough of the bunch, haven't you? After all, I'm not such a bad catch myself. My father doesn't do so bad with twenty thousand bucks a year."

"Well," I changed the subject," are you really having any fun here? It feels like a morgue to me. Lets get some liquor and scram. These damn monkey-suits kill me."

"Do you think Dexter will like it?"

"I think Dexter has something better to do to keep him busy besides worry about us."

"And your latest heart-throbs - do you

think they'll come just like that?"

"Dick knows them," I said, giving him a
sideward glance.

Dick, a bit more alive than usual, gave
himself a slap on the thigh.

"Lee, you sure know your onions. Now
you're cooking on the front burner."

"I thought I was a longhair!"

"Must be a wig."

"Go after those two babes," I said, "and
drag them over. Or rather, try to get them into
my car, or in yours if you like."

"But what'll I use for an excuse?"

"Come on, Dick," I told him, "Can
you use your head for something besides a
hatrack? You can sure dig up
something from your long experience to get
them along!"

He took off, shaking his head, but
laughing. Jicky had been listening and now
took on a mocking smile. I beckoned to her
and she came over.

"How about you chasing after Judy and
Bill, and getting about seven or eight pints or
so?"

"Where we going to go?"

"Where can we go to?"

"My father and mother aren't home,"
said Jicky, "Just my little brother and he'll be

sleeping. Come to my house."

"You're a peach, Jicky. Cross your heart."

She lowered her voice.

"Will you do it to me?"

"What!?"

"Will you, Lee?"

"Oh! Sure thing," I said.

Though I'd had Jicky often enough, I think I could have laid her on the spot. It was very exciting to see her in her evening dress with her shock of smooth hair hanging down her left cheek, her slightly slanty eyes and her ingenue mouth. She was breathing faster and her cheeks had become red.

"It's silly maybe, Lee. I know we do it all the time... But I like it so much!"

"O.K., Jicky," I said, stroking her shoulder, "Don't worry, we'll have another go at least once before we kick off."

She pressed my wrist very hard, and then went off before I could stop her. I felt like telling her then and there, tell her what I was, just to see her face... but Jicky wasn't worth wasting that on. I felt as strong as John Henry and I didn't have to worry about my heart breaking.

I went back to the bar and asked the one serving for a double martini. I tossed it off in a

gulp and then decided to do something to help
out Dick.

I saw the older Asquith girl come
over near there. She was chatting with Dexter.
I liked his looks even less than usual with his
black lock of hair hanging down his forehead.
His tux fitted him just right. He almost looked
well built because of it, and his dark tan
against the white shirt made a good ad for the
Hotel Splendide in Bermuda.

I went straight up to them.

"Dex," I said, "would you mind very
much if I asked Miss Asquith for this dance?"

"I guess you're too big for me, Lee,"
Dexter replied. "I won't fight."

I don't think he really gave a hang, but
you never could tell exactly what that guy
meant anyhow. I had already put my arms
around Jean Asquith.

I think I still preferred her sister
Lou. I would never have thought there was a
difference of five years between them. Jean
was almost as tall as I am. She was at least
four inches taller than Lou. Her gown consist-
ed of two pieces of some black and very trans-
parent fabric, the lower part in several thick-
nesses. She had on a very complicated looking brassiere which nevertheless covered a
minimum of flesh. She had a golden skin,

with some freckles on her shoulders and forehead, and her hair, done up in a very short
permanent, gave her head a rather roundish
appearance. She also had a rounder face
than Lou.

"Are you having any fun here?" I
asked her.

"Oh, parties are all alike. This one isn't
any worse than any other."

"Right now," I said, "I find it much better than any other."

She was a very good dancer. It was
very easy for me. And then too, I had no reason for not holding her closer than her sister,
since she could talk to me without looking up
to me. She pressed her cheek against mine;
when I lowered my eyes a little they fell on her
nicely rounded ear, her funny short hair and
her round shoulder. She smelt of sage and
wild herbs.

"What perfume do you use?" I went on,
since she hadn't answered.

"I never use any perfume," she said.

I didn't want to keep this kind of
chitchat up for ever, so I decided to take a
chance and act.

"How'd you like to go somewhere
where we could really have some fun."

"For example?"

She spoke with a rather nonchalant air, without raising her head, and what she said seemed to come from behind me.

"Oh, a place where you can drink all you want, smoke all you want, and where you have all the room you want to dance in."

"That would be something," she said. "The way we've been dancing you'd think we were doing some Balinese number."

As a matter of fact we hadn't been able to move a bit in the last five minutes and had just been moving our feet back and forth in time with the music and not covering any ground at all. I loosened my grip on her but still keeping my arm around her waist, I guided her out.

"Well, let's go," I said. "We'll go over to my friends place."

I turned my head to her at the instant she said that and caught her breath right in my face. God knows I'm not lying when I say she had killed at least half a quart of gin.

"Just who are these friends of yours?"

"Oh, they're very nice," I assured her.

We were going through the empty vestibule. I didn't bother to get her cape. The air was warm and scented by the jasmine on the porch.

"After all," Jean said as we stopped at

the portico, "I hardly know you."

"Of course you do," I said carrying her
along, "I'm you're old friend, Lee Anderson."

She broke out into an uncontrolled
laugh and let herself be taken along.

"Oh, to be sure, Lee Anderson. Come
along Lee, everybody's waiting for us."

I now had a tough time keeping up
with her. She raced down the porch steps and
I didn't catch up with her until we'd both covered about thirty feet.

"Hold it," I said, "not so fast!"

I got a good hold on her.

"The car is over that way."

Judy and Bill were waiting in the Nash.

"We've got some liquor," Judy whispered. Dick is just ahead of us with the others."

"Lou Asquith too,?" I murmured.

"Yes, Don Juan, she's there too. You
can take off now."

Jean Asquith with her head flopped on
the back of the front seat stretched out an
uncertain hand to Bill.

"Hiya, how do you do? Is it raining?"

"Don't be a sill," Bill caught on,
"The bottom of the barometer dropped out but

that's tomorrow's weather, not today's."

"Oh," said Jean. "I don't think your car'll ever make it."

"Don't be slandering my Rolls-Royce." I protested, "Do you feel cold?"

I bent over her to look for a blanket I knew didn't exist, "accidentally" hooking my jacket buttons on her skirt and lifting it over her knees. Glory! What legs!

"I'm dying from the heat," Jean said in an unsteady voice.

I let out the clutch and followed Dick's car, which had just set out in front of us. There was a whole row of cars of various swank makes in front of Dexter's house, and I would have liked to take one of them instead of my decrepit Nash. But I'd manage even without a new car.

Jicky didn't live very far away, in a colonial-style house. The garden, surrounded by a rather high hedge, was quite nicer than the rest in the neighborhood.

I saw Dick's stop-light stop moving and then go out; then his parking lights went on. I stopped my car as I heard the roadster's door slam. Four people had gotten out : Dick, Jicky, Lou, and somebody else. From the way he went up the porch steps I guessed it was Shorty Nick. He and Dick each had a couple of bottles and I then saw that Judy and Bill also had some. Jean Asquith didn't seem to want to get out of the car, so I got out, walked around it to her side, opened the door, slipped one arm under her knees and another under her neck. She got a bang on the nose in the process. Judy came up behind me.

"She's groggy, your nice little girl-friend. What did you do, hit her?"

"I don't know if it was me or the gin she drank," I muttered, "maybe she's just having a beauty nap."

"Now's the time to take advantage of her, cuty-pie. Go to it."

"Oh go lay an egg. It's too easy with somebody that's drunk."

"Hey you!"

It was Jean's pleasant voice. She was coming to.

"Lemme down!"

I saw that she was going to throw up, so I jumped into Jicky's garden. Judy went up and closed the door, and I held Jean's head while she went at it. It was a fine mess. Gin, plain, and unadulterated. And as hard to keep down as an unbroken colt. She did a thorough job. I held her up with one hand.

"Roll my sleeve up," I whispered to Judy.

She rolled the sleeve of my tux up my arm, and I maneuvered myself so as to hold Miss Asquith on the other side. "Now, go to it," said Judy, when Jean was finished. "I'll lay chicky. Take your time." Bill had long since disappeared with his bottles.

"Where can you get water?" I asked Judy.

"In the house. Come on, we'll go in the back way."

I followed her through the garden, half dragging Jean, who stumbled at each step she took on the gravel path. Lord, she was heavy! She was quite a handful. Judy went ahead of me on the staircase and led me upstairs. The rest of the gang was making a big racket in the living room. Fortunately the door was closed and muffled the noise. I groped my way up in the dark, keeping my eyes on Judy's behind which reflected light from somewhere. At the top of the staircase she managed to find a switch, and I went into the bathroom. There was a big rubber bath-mat along side the tub.

"Put her on that," Judy said.

"No fooling around," I said. "Take off her skirt."

She unzipped it and took off the frilly stuff in a jiffy. She rolled her stockings down to her ankles. I've got to say that I never really knew what a good figure was until I saw Jean Asquith lying nude on that mat. She was something to look at. Her eyes were closed, and her mouth was still somewhat frothy. I wiped it with a bit of Kleenex. Not so much for her sake, as for mine. Judy was busy rummaging through the medicine chest.

"I've got just the thing, Lee," she finally said. "Make her drink this."

"She can't drink now. She's sleeping. She hasn't got a thing in her stomach."

"Well then, do it now, Lee. Don't mind me. When she wakes up maybe she won't want to."

"Take it easy, Judy."

"Maybe it bothers you that I've got my clothes on."

She went to the door and turned the bolt. And then she took off her dress and her bra leaving nothing but her stockings.

"Up to you, Lee."

She sat down on the edge of the bathtub, her legs spread apart, and looked at me. I couldn't hold myself back any longer. I ripped my clothes off.

"Get down on top of her, Lee. Get the lead out of your pants."

"Judy," I said. "You're disgusting."

"Why? I think it'll be fun to see you on her. Come on, Lee, do something..."

I dropped down on Jean, but that damn Judy had taken the breath out of me. I didn't have any more power. I remained on my knees with Jean between my legs. Judy came over to me again. I felt her hand guide me to the proper place. She didn't take her hand away. I almost cried out she got me so excited. Jean didn't budge-then I looked at her face and saw she was dribbling again. She had half-opened her eyes, and then closed them again, and I felt that she was beginning to move a bit, swaying her back. Meanwhile Judy continued her guidance, and with her other hand, caressed my behind.

Judy got up. She went over to the switch and turned the light off. It was too much even for her under the bright light. She came back to me and I thought she was going to do the same thing, but this time she bent over me and gave me a feel. I was still in the same position, and she stretched out on her belly on top of me, but head to toe, and now instead of her hand, I felt her mouth.

Boris Vian

VI

I finally decided, after about an hour, that the others would begin to wonder about us so, I crawled out from between them. I can't recall in just what part of the master bathroom we ended up in.

I was a little dizzy and had an aching back. And my thighs were pretty chewed up where Jean's nails had given me a good raking. I crawled over to the wall and got myself organized and then found the switch. Judy had begun to stir. I put the lights on and saw her sitting on the ground, rubbing her eyes. Jean was on her belly on the bath mat, her head resting on her arm. She looked as though she were asleep. God she had a beautiful back! I quickly put my shirt and my pants back on. Judy was touching herself up before the washbasin. I took a face cloth and wet it. I lifted her head to awaken her and found her eyes wide open, and she was even laughing. I caught her around the waist and sat her down on the edge of the tub.

"What you need is a good shower."

"I'm too tired," she said. "I guess I drank a little."

"You can say that again," Judy broke in.

"Oh, not so much," I reassured her.

-54-

"You'll be alright again with a little nap."

Then she got up and hooked her arm around my neck, and gave me a long kiss. I worked myself slowly out of her embrace, and put her in the tub.

"Close your eyes and lift your head up."

I turned the hot and cold faucets and the shower struck her in the face. She stretched out her body under the warm water and I could see the nipples of her breasts become darker and jut out a bit.

"Mmm, that's good."

Judy was rolling up her stockings.

"Step on it, you two. If we go down right away maybe we'll still be able to get something to drink."

I got a huge bath towel. Jean shut off the faucets and I wrapped her n the fluffy fabric. She sure liked the way it felt.

"Where are we," she asked. "In Dexter's house?"

"No, at some friend's," I replied.
"We were having too boring a time to stay at Dexter's."

"I'm glad you brought me along," she said. "It won't be so stuffy here."

She was all dry by now. I handed her both parts of her gown.

"Get it on," I said, "Fix up your face and

come on downstairs."

I went towards the door. I opened it for Judy who raced down the steps. I was going to follow her.

"Wait for me, Lee..."

Jean turned her back for me to hook up her brassiere. I tenderly bit the nape of her neck. She leaned over backwards.

"Will you sleep with me again?"

"And how," I said. "Any time you say."

"Right away?"

"Your sister is going to wonder where you are."

"Lou's here?"

"Of course!"

"Oh! Well, that's very nice," said Jean. "Now I'll be able to chaperone her."

"I don't think your chaperoning her will do her much good," I said.

"How do you like her, Lee?"

"I wouldn't mind sleeping with her either," I said.

She laughed again.

"I think she's wonderful. I wish I looked like her. If you only saw her naked."

"How abut fixing me up?"

"Really, now, don't be such a leech!"

"Pardon ME! I didn't have the opportunity to learn proper etiquette."

"I think your manners are very nice,' she said, looking at me invitingly.

I placed my arm around her waist and led her to the door.

"It's about time we went down."

"I like your voice very much too."

"Come on."

"Would you want to marry me."

"Don't talk nonsense!"

I started to go down the staircase.

"I'm not talking nonsense! You've got to marry me now."

She looked quite calm and sure of what she was saying.

"I can't marry you!"

"Why not?"

"Because I think I'd rather have your sister."

She laughed again.

"Oh, Lee, I'm crazy about you."

"Thank you," I said.

Everybody was in the living room, making a big racket. I pushed the door open and let Jean go in before me. Our coming was greeted by a chorus of catcalls. They'd opened some canned chicken and were stuffing it away like little pigs. Bill, Dick and Nicholas were in their shirtsleeves, and had gravy all over their clothes. Lou had an enormous spot of mayonnaise on her dress, running down its full length. And Judy and Jicky were just gorging themselves without a care in the world. I noticed that at least five of the bottles were almost empty.

The radio was giving out monotonously and without too much volume a program of dance music.

When she got near the chicken, Jean let out an Indian war-whoop and grabbed a big chunk into which she sank her teeth without further ado. I fixed myself up, filling my plate.

Things were going very well,I thought.

VII

At three o'clock in the morning, Dexter called up. Jean was doing a good job getting herself another drunk on, even better than the first one, and I took advantage of that to latch her onto Nicholas. I didn't leave her sister, however, -

I rather plied her with drinks, as much as I could, but she offered a lot of resistance and it wasn't easy. Dexter warned us that Mr. and Mrs. Asquith were beginning to wonder what had happened to their daughters. I asked him how come he knew where we were, and he just laughed over the phone. I told him why we, had skipped out.

"That's O.K., Lee," he said, "I know you couldn't have had any fun at my place tonight. Too many good people."

"How about you coming over too, Dex," I suggested.

"What's the matter, no more liquor?"

"No, it isn't that," I protested. "But you'll get a new slant on things here."

He was caustic as usual, though his tone of voice remained perfectly innocent.

"I can't get away from here, he said. "Otherwise I'd come over. What should I tell the girl's parents."

Boris Vian

"Tell them we'll deliver their little girls
to their very door."
"I don't think they're going to like that,
Lee. You know..."
"Oh, they're old enough to take care of
themselves."
"Yeah, but they know they're not alone."
"Fix it up, Dex old pal. I'm counting
on you."
"O.K. Lee, I'll take care of it. See you
later."
"So long."
He hung up. I did too, and went back
to my campaign. Jicky and Bill were begin-
ning to indulge in some exer-
cises not intended for young ladies of
good family, and I was curious to see how Lou
would react. She had finally let herself take
some drinks. She didn't seem to be very
shocked, even when Bill started taking Judy's
dress off.
"What'll you have?"
"Whisky."
"Toss it down, and we'll dance."
I took hold of her and tried to take her
into another room.
"What do you want to do in there."
"Too much noise here."
She followed me without a word. She

sat down on a divan next to me without any protest, but when I tried to pet her, I got a slap as startling as the one I got the day I was born. I was mad as hell, but I managed to keep smiling.

"Put your paws down," Lou said.

"You're a pretty tough baby,' I commented.

"Well you started it!"

"That's no excuse. Do you think this is a Sunday-school class? Or a bingo party?"

"Oh, I just don't feel like being first prize."

"That's what you are, whether you like it or not."

"I suppose you're thinking of my father's fortune."

"No, - I'm thinking of this."

I pushed her back onto the divan and tore at the front of her dress. She fought like a wildcat. Her breasts popped out of the sheer silk.

"Let me go! You're just a big brute!"

"No," I said, "I'm a man."

"You're disgusting," she said as she tried to break away. "What did you do that whole hour you spent upstairs with Jean?"

"Nothing at all," I said. "You know very well Judy was with us."

"I'm beginning to understand just what kind of a crowd this is, Lee Anderson, and what kind of people you are."

"Lou, I swear that I didn't touch your sister except to sober her up."

"You're lying. Didn't you see the way she looked at you when she came down again?"

"Well, I'll be...! Sound so as though you're jealous."

She looked at me with stupefaction.

"Well! And just who and what do you think you are!"

"Do you think that I'd still want to do something to you if I had touched your sister?"

"Well she isn't any better than I am!"

I was still holding her down on the divan. She'd stopped struggling. Her breasts rose and fell rhythmically. I bent over her and kissed them with long kisses, one after the other, caressing the nipples with my tongue. Then I stood up.

"No Lou," I said. "She isn't any better than you are."

I let her go and stepped back quickly, since I expected a violent reaction. But she turned over on her side and began to cry.

VIII

After the party, I went back to my everyday work. I'd set the trap - I now had to wait for events to take their course. I knew I 'd see them again. I didn't think Jean would forget me after seeing how'd she'd looked at me, and as for Lou, I counted on her very youngness, and also on what I'd said and done to her in Jicky's house.

The following week I got in a big shipment of new books that announced the end of autumn and the beginning of the winter season. I kept up my good work, and I was able to put quite a few dollars away. I now had a pretty good sum. Nothing much, really, but it would be enough. I had to make some expenditures. Get some new clothes, and have my car overhauled. A couple of times I'd substituted for the guitarist in the only fairly decent orchestra in town, the one that played at the Stork Club. I don't think this Stork Club had any connection with the New York one, but the solid young gentlemen with glasses were glad to come there with the daughters of insurance agents or of tractor salesmen. I earned some extra dough that way, and also got to know people who came to buy books from me. The fellows and girls from our bunch sometimes went there too. I still saw them regularly, and I still kept laying Judy and Jicky. I couldn't get rid of Jicky. It was lucky I had both of them, though, for I was in rare form. In addition to all that, I took part in various sports, and developed the muscles of a prizefighter.

And then, one evening, about a week after the party which began at Dex's house, I got a letter from Tom. He asked me to come as quickly as possible. I took advantage of the weekend and went down to where he was. I knew Tom hadn't written me for no good reason, and I suspected it wasn't about something pleasant.

There'd been some fights in connection with the elections, stirred up by Senator Balbo, the biggest bastard in the state. Ever since the colored men had been trying to vote, he'd been stirring up hell. He managed it so that a couple of days before the election, some of his men broke up some colored meetings, beating a couple of men to death.

My brother, who was a teacher in the colored school had made a public protest, and had sent a letter on the subject, and the next day, they beat him up too. He'd written me to come and get him with the car, to take him somewhere else.

He was waiting for me in our house, all

alone in the dark room. He was sitting on a
chair when I came in. It hurt me to see his
broad but bent back and the way he held his
head in his hands. I felt my blood, my good
Negro blood, throb in anger through my veins
and sing in my ears. He got up and took me
by the shoulders. His mouth was swollen and
he could speak but with pain. When I was
about to give him a slap on the back to cheer
him up he caught my arm.

"They bullwhipped me," he said.

"Who did it?"

"Bleb's gang. The Moran boy."

"That guy again!"

My fists balled up involuntarily. A bit-
ter anger came over me.

"Do you want me to knock him off,
Tom?"

"No, Lee. We couldn't. They'd kill you.
You've still got a chance, Lee, you haven't got
any of the signs."

"But you're a better man than I am,
Tom."

"Just look at my hands, Lee. Look at my
nails. And my hair and my lips. I'm black,
Lee. I can't get away from it. But you !..."

He stopped talking and just looked at
me. He really loved me.

"You, Lee, you ought to get away from
it. God will help you to. He'll help you, Lee."
"God doesn't give a hang," I said.
He smiled. He knew I had no more reli-
gion.
"Lee, you were too young when you left
this town, and you've lost your religion, but
God will forgive you when the time comes.
Flee from men. But come to Him, with open
arms and open heart."
"Where are you going to go, Tom? Do
you need any money?"
"I've got money, Lee. I wanted to leave
the house together with you. I want to..."
He stopped. The words came with dif-
ficulty from his twisted mouth.
"I want to burn the house down, Lee.
Our father built it. We owe everything to him.
His skin was almost that of a white man, Lee.
But he never thought of going back on his
race-remember, Lee? Our brother is dead, and
nobody shall live in the house our father built
with his own black hands."
I said nothing. I helped Tom get his
things together and we piled it into the Nash.
The house was situated out on the edge of
town, in a rather isolated spot. I left Tom to
finish up in the house, and I went over to the
car to do over the bundles.

He joined me a couple of minutes later.
"Well," he said, "Let's get going. We've
got to go away because the time when there
will be equal justice for the black man as well
as the white man is not yet at hand."

A red light flickered in the kitchen, and
then suddenly flashed brightly. We heard the
muffled roar of an exploding gas-can and then
the bright gleam reached the window of the
adjoining room. And finally a tongue of
flame cut through the board wall, and the
wind fanned the flame. The fire danced about
and Tom's face, in the bright red light, shone
with sweat. Two heavy tears rolled down his
cheeks. And he placed his hand on my shoulder and we turned our backs on the scene.

I'm pretty sure Tom could have sold the
house. With the money he could have caused
the Morans a good bit of trouble, maybe even
knock off a couple of them, but I didn't want to
stop him from doing what he thought he
ought to do. And I did what I thought I had to
do. He still had a lot of funny ideas about
kindness and godliness in his head. He was
too honest, Tom was, and that's what ruined
him. He thought that if he were good and
kind, he would be repaid with kindness but it
was quite rare that things turned out so. There
is only one thing that matters, and that is to

have revenge, full and complete revenge. I thought of the kid, who had been even whiter than I was, if that were possible. When Anne Moran's father had learned that he was going with his daughter, all hell broke loose.

But the kid had never left our town, whereas I had been away for more than ten years, in contact with people who didn't know what I came from, and I had been able to lose that abject humility that grows upon us, bit by bit, like a reflex; that hateful humility which made Tom's torn lips proffer words of compassion; the fright which made my brothers hide themselves every time they heard a white man's footsteps. But I knew that if we only had his skin we'd be ahead of him, for he talks too much and betrays his weaknesses when he's in the company of what he thinks are other white men.

With Bill, with Dick, and with Judy, I'd already gotten several points up on them. But I didn't think it worth while telling them a "nigger" had taken them-I wouldn't get what I really wanted that way. I'd have my revenge on Moran and on every last one of them when I'd done with Lou and Jean Asquith. Two at a clip, and they wouldn't get me like they did my brother.

Tom was dozing away in the car. I stepped on the gas. I had to take him to the main line stop at Murchison Junction, where he'd take the streamliner up North. He'd decided to go back to New York. He was a nice guy, Tom was. A nice guy but too sentimental. Too meek and resigned.

IX

I got back to town the next morning and went back to work without having slept at all. I wasn't sleepy. I was still waiting. It finally came about eleven o'clock in the shape of a phone-call. Jean Asquith invited me and Dex and other friends up to her place for the week-end. I accepted of course, but tried not to appear too eager.

"I'll try," I said.

"Please come," she urged me.

"You don't need men that bad, do you," I kidded her. "Or are you really out in the desert there."

"The men around here don't know what to do with a girl that's had too much to drink."

That left me cold. I guess she felt it, cause I heard a little burst of laughter.

"Really do come, Lee. I want to see you. And Lou will be glad too."

"Give her a kiss for me,' I said, "and tell her to give you a kiss for me too."

I went back to work feeling better. My morale was up. That night I went to the drug store to meet the gang, and then I took Judy and Jicky in my Nash. Maybe a car isn't the most comfortable place in the world, but you can always find a new angle. That was another night I slept well.

Next morning, to fill in some things I needed, I went and bought a set of toilet articles and brushes in a leather case, a valise, a new pair of pajamas, and some other little items I didn't have. I didn't want them to think I was a nobody, and I knew just about what was needed to keep from giving that impression.

Thursday evening that week, I was just finishing my records for the day and filling in the necessary forms when, around half past five, I saw Dex's car stop out at the curb. I had already locked up so I went to open up for him and he came in.

"Hiya, Lee," he called out to me, "How's things?"

"Not bad, Dex. And how's your school-work?"

"Oh, I manage. I'm not enough of an athlete to make a real first class alma mater man, you know."

"What brings you around?"

"Oh, I thought I'd take you out to supper somewhere and then take you along to see how you like some of my favorite amusements."

"Thanks, Dex. Just give me about five minutes."

"I'll wait out in the car."

I stuffed my forms and the cash into the safe, pulled over the iron grillwork and then went out the back way carrying my jacket on my arm. It was very sticky, much too hot for that late date. The heavy, moist air made everything stick to your skin.

"Should I take the guitar along?" I asked Dex.

"No, not necessary. Tonight I'll arrange the amusements."

"Okey Doke."

I got in up front, next to him. There was no comparison between his Packard and my Nash, but he just didn't know how to drive. You've got to be really lousy to race the motor of a Packard "Clipper" in low gear.

"Where are you taking me, Dex?"

"First we'll go eat at the Stork, and then I'll take you where we're going."

"I guess you're going up to the Asquiths Saturday, aren't you."

"Yep. I'll take you along, if you like."

In that way I wouldn't have to show up in my Nash. A front like Dexter was always a good bet.

"Thanks. Glad to."

"Do you play golf, Lee?"

"I've tried it just once."

"Have you got the right clothes, and a set of clubs?"

"Of course not. Who do you think I am, J.P. Morgan?"

"The Asquiths have a private links. I'd advise you to say your doctor ordered you not to play."

"Do you think anybody'd believe that?" I muttered.

"And how about bridge."

"Oh, pretty fair."

"Fair, or good?"

"Just fair."

"Then I'd suggest you say that bridge is bad for your heart or something."

"But after all," I insisted, "I can play..."

"Yes, but can you afford to drop five hundred bucks just like that?"

"That wouldn't be so nice."

"Then you'd better follow my advice."

"You're just full of nice suggestions tonight, Dex." I said. "If you took me along tonight just to let me know that I'm too damn broke to go visit those people, just say so and I'll get out."

"I think you'd do better to thank me than get huffed up, Lee. All I'm doing is giving you some advice that might help you put up the proper show when you do go visit those people, as you call them."

"I wonder why it concerns you so much."

"Oh, it interests me."

He said nothing for a moment as he suddenly braked for a red light. The Packard swung us forth on it's springs for an instant, and then settled back.

"I don't see just what interests you."

"I'm just wondering what you intend to do with those girls."

"Any good-looking girl is worth doing something with."

"You've got dozens of girls at your feet who are just as good-looking, and much easier to get."

"I don't think you're right on the first account," I said, "nor, as a matter of fact, on the second."

He gave me a look as though he were cooking up something. I liked it better when he kept his eyes on the road.

"You surprise me, Lee."

"Frankly," I said, "those two girls are just what I go for."

"Yes, I know that's just what you like," Dex said. I was sure that wasn't all that he meant.

"I don't think it should be any harder to

lay them than either Judy or Jicky," I said.

"Is that all you're after, Lee?"

"Just that!"

"Well all I can say is you'd better look out. I don't know just what you did to Jean, but talking with her just about five minutes on the phone, she managed to mention your name at least four times."

"Well, I guess I made quite an impression on her."

"They're not the kind of girls you can lay unless you marry them. At least I think they're like that. You know, Lee, I've known the family for all of ten years."

"Well then, I guess I can call myself lucky,' I replied, "because I don't expect to marry both of them and I can tell you right now that I expect to lay both of them."

Dexter didn't say another word, but just looked at me. I wondered if Judy had told him about our business at Jicky's house, or didn't he know a thing. I felt that he was quite capable of guessing lots of things you didn't tell him and didn't want him to know.

"O.K., you can get out now," he said.

I suddenly realized that we had stopped in front of the Stork Club, and I got out.

Dexter followed me in, and we left our hats with the check girl. A waiter in formal dress who I knew quite well led us to our reserved table. They tried to imitate big-town style in this joint, and sometimes it was very funny. I stopped to say hello to Blackie, the band-leader, as we passed. Lots of people were having cocktails and the band was play-ing some dance-music. I knew most of the customers by sight. But I was used to seeing them from the orchestra platform and I now got that usual funny feeling I got when I was on the other side of the fence, with them.

We sat down, and Dex ordered a couple of double Martinis.

"Lee," he said, "I don't want to talk about it any more so I'll just say once and for, look out for those girls."

"I'm always careful," I said. "I don't know just how you meant that, but in general I know just what I'm doing."

He didn't reply to that. Two minutes later he started talking about something else. When he let himself drop his supercilious manner, he could really be an interesting talk-er.

X

Both of us were pretty well tanked up by the time we got out, and I took the wheel over Dexter's protestations.

"I just want to make sure I still have my pretty face for next Saturday. You never look at the road when you drive, and I always feel that we're going to hit something."

"But you don't know the way, Lee."

"So what!" I said, "You can tell me where to turn."

"It's in a part of the town you've never seen, and it's pretty complicated."

"Oh, don't be silly, Dex. What's the name of the street?"

"Well, OK. Take us to the thirteen hundred block on Stephen Street."

"It's over there, isn't it?" I asked, pointing vaguely in the direction of the western end of town.

"Yeah,- you know where it is?"

"There's lots of things I know," I told him. "Hold tight, I'm taking off."

The Packard was a joy to drive. Dex didn't think much of it and would rather have had his old-man's Cadillac. But compared to my Nash, it was a honey.

"The place we're going to is right on Stephen Street?"

"Near by," Dex said.

In spite of the heavy drinking we'd been doing he looked pretty sober. You could hardly tell he'd had anything.

We ended up right in the middle of the rundown part of town. Stephen Street started out all right, but after about number 200 or so we ran into some chap boarding houses, then some one-story shacks, looking more miserable the farther we went. When we reached 1300, they looked as though they could hardly keep standing. There were some old jalopies parked about, mostly model T Fords. I stopped Dex's car where he told me to.

"Come on, Lee," he said. "We'll do a stretch on foot."

He locked the car and we started out. He turned down a side street and we covered a couple of hundred feet. There were scraggly trees and tumble-down fences about. Dex stopped in front of a two-story structure, the top half of which was made of rough boards. The iron fence, surrounding a mass of debris which constituted the garden was miraculously in fairly good condition. He went in without ringing. It was almost dark already and peculiar shadows gave an eerie aspect to the place.

"Come on, Lee," he said. "This is it."

"I'm coming."

There was a rosebush in front of the house, just one, but its perfume was enough to mitigate the unpleasantness of the garbage that was lying about on all sides. Dex hopped up the two steps leading into the house on the side. A fat colored woman answered when he rang. She turned around without a word and Dex followed. I shut the door behind me.

On the first floor she stood aside to let us pass. We went into a little room with a couch, a bottle and a couple of glasses, and two little girls about eleven or twelve years old. One of them was a red-head, chubby and very freckled. The other a colored girl, a little older than the other, it seemed to me.

They were sitting very properly on the couch, both dressed in a blouse and a very short skirt.

"Here are some gentlemen who will give you some money," said the colored woman. "Be very nice to them."

She shut the door, leaving us alone. I looked at Dexter.

"Take your clothes off, Lee," he said, "it's very hot in here."

He turned to the red-head.

"Come and help me, Jo."

"My name's Polly," the child said. "Are you going to give me some dollars?"

"Sure, sure," Dex said.

He took a crumpled ten out of his pocket and gave it to the girl.

"Come and help me take my pants off."

I hadn't even moved. I watched the red-head get up. She must have been a little bit over twelve years old. Her can was nicely rounded under her too short skirt. I knew that Dex was looking at me.

"I'll take the red-head," he said.

"You know that they're jail bait, don't you?"

"Maybe it's the dark meat that's bothering you!" he said harshly.

So that's what he was driving at. He was still looking at me, with his damn lock of hair hanging down over his eye. He was just waiting for me to say or do something. I think I didn't show anything. The two kids just sat there, a bit terrified.

"Come on, Polly," Dex finally said. "How about a little drink."

"No please, thank you,' she said. "I can help you without drinking."

In less than a minute he had his clothes off and had taken the child on his knees and lifted up her skirt. His face had become flushed, and he was breathing harder.

"You're not going to hurt me, are you?" she said.

"You keep quiet," Dexter replied, "Or you don't get any money."

He pushed his hands between her legs and she began to cry.

"Shut up!" he cried, "Or I'll make Anna beat you."

He turned his head toward me. I still hadn't moved.

"Is it the dark meat that's bothering you," he said again. "Would you rather have this one?"

"No, it's alright this way,' I said.

I looked at the other girl. She was scratching her head, quite indifferent to what was going on. Her body had already taken the shape of a woman.

"Come over here," I said to her.

"You can let yourself go, Lee. They're clean," he said to me. Then, to the girl: "You stop that whimpering!"

Polly stopped crying and just sniffled for a while.

"You're too big for me," she said, "That hurts!"

"You keep quiet," Dex said, "And I'll

give you another five dollars."

He was panting like a dog on a hot day. He grabbed her by the thighs and moved rhythmically on the chair.

Polly's tears rolled down without a sound. The little colored girl looked at me.

"Take your clothes off," I said to her, "and lie down on the couch."

I took my jacket off, and loosened my belt. She uttered a slight cry when I went into her. She was as hot as an oven.

XI

Saturday came, and I hadn't seen Dexter
again all week. I decided to take my Nash and
go as far as his place with it. If he was going
too, I'd leave it in his garage. Otherwise I'd
use my own car.

He was as sick as a dog when I left him
that evening. He must have been a lot drunker
than I thought, cause he started pulling some
funny tricks. Little Polly would probably
always have a scar on her left breast because
the hound had gotten it into his head to bite a
chunk out of her. He thought his money
would be able to calm her down, but when the
colored woman Anna ran back in, she threat-
ened to never let him come again. I was sure it
wasn't the first time he'd come to that place.
He didn't want to let Polly go-I think the
smell of her freckled skin had a special effect
on him. Anna put a sort of bandage on her,
and gave her a sleeping pill, but she had to
leave her with Dex, who tongued her from top
to bottom, uttering some strange sounds from
his throat.

I could guess what he felt like, since, as
far as I was concerned, I could hardly get
myself to get out of that little black girl. Still, I
tried not to hurt her in any way, and she didn't

complain even once. She just closed her eyes.

That was why I wondered whether Dexter would be back in shape by Saturday for the trip to the Asquiths. I myself was not quite myself when I got up after that night. I went to Ricardo's to recover: at nine in the morning he served me a double Zombie and that's enough to put anybody back in shape. I'd never done much drinking before I came to Buckton, and I now realized what a mistake that had been. All you've got to do is drink enough, - there's nothing that'll straighten out your head as well as that. That morning everything went fine, and when I stopped in front of Dex's house, I was in rare form.

Contrary to my expectations, he was all ready for me, freshly shaven, dressed in a light gabardine suit, and a swank, sharpy shirt.

"Did you eat yet, Lee? I hate stopping on the road, so I'd prefer to get that over with now."

In some ways, Dexter was as simple, clear and innocent as a kid. But maybe a kid who knew too much for his years. His eyes showed it.

"I wouldn't mind some ham and eggs, and maybe some bread and jam," I replied.

The butler served me well. I hate to have a man stick his hands on everything I eat, but it seemed quite natural to Dexter.

We left right after I'd eaten. I carried my things from the Nash to the Packard, and Dexter got in on the right.

"You drive, Lee. That's a good idea."

He gave me a side glance. That was his only reference to that night. The rest of the way he was in excellent good humor and told me a lot of stories about Mr. and Mrs. Asquith, a fine pair of crooks who had inherited a lot of money, which is alright, but they used it to exploit people whose only crime is that they have a different color skin than theirs. They owned a flock of sugar-cane plantations in the West Indies and, according to Dex, all they ever drank in their place was rum.

"That's as good as Ricardo's Zombies any day, Lee."

"Well then I'll have no kick to make," I replied.

And I pressed even harder on the gas pedal.

It didn't take that car much more than an hour to make the hundred miles to Prixville, and Dexter directed me once we got there. It was a little town, not as big as Buckton, but the houses were swankier and their grounds bigger. There are towns like that, where everybody seems to be in the upper brackets.

The big gate to the grounds was open and I went up the driveway to the garage in second, but with no complaint from the motor as when Dex was driving. I pulled the Clipper in behind two other cars.

"Some of the other customers are here already," I said.

"No," Dex informed me. "They belong to the Asquiths. I think we're the first ones. Besides us there'll just be some local people. They take turns inviting each other, because they get bored to death in their own houses. They try to get away from them as much as possible."

"Yeah," I said dryly, "they must have a rough time."

He laughed and got out. We both grabbed our bags and turned around to find ourselves face to face with Jean Asquith. She was carrying a tennis racket. She had on white shorts and also an azure blue pullover which I guess she'd put on after her last set. It was a very tight fit and she stuck out to a startling degree.

"Oh, so here you are," she said.

She seemed to be delighted to see us.

"Come on and have some refresments."

I looked at Dex, and he looked at me,

and we both nodded approvingly in concert.

"Where's Lou?" Dex asked.

"She went up already. She's got to change."

"Oh," I said, suspiciously. "You dress for bridge here?"

Jean burst into laughter.

"I meant she had to change shorts. You can go put on something more comfortable than that and then come down again. I'll have somebody show you to your rooms."

"I hope you're going to change shorts too," I kidded her. You must have those on for at least an hour."

She gave me a swift cut across my fingers with the racket.

"I don't sweat like her!" Jean asserted. "I'm too old for that."

"And I suppose you lost the match, didn't you?"

"Uh-huh!"

She laughed again. She knew she looked good when she laughed.

"In that case," said Dex, "Maybe I can take a chance and ask you to play a set with me. Not right away, of course. Tomorrow morning."

"Sure thing," Jean said.

Maybe I'm wrong, but I think she

would have been gladder if it were me.

"O.K.," I said. "If there are two courts, I'll play a set with Lou and the two losers will take each other on. Make sure you lose, and then we'll be able to play together."

"O.K.," Jean said.

"Well," Dex concluded, "If everybody is going to cheat, I'm sure to lose."

We all broke into a laugh. It wasn't funny; but the situation had become forced, and it had to be smoothed out. Dex and I then followed Jean to the house, where a colored chambermaid, very slender and with a little starched white bonnet took us over.

XII

I changed up in my room, and then
went down to Dex and the others. There were
two other fellows and two girls, evenly paired
off, and Jean was playing bridge with one of
the girls and the two boys. Lou was there too.
I left the other girl to Dex and I turned the
radio on to find a bit of dance-music. I got a
Stan Kenton program and left it there. It was
better than nothing. Lou had used a new perfume, one I liked better than that of the other
time, but I wanted to tease her.

"New perfume, Lou?"

"Yes. Don't like it?"

"It's all right. But I suppose you know
that that just isn't done."

"What?"

"You're not supposed to change perfumes. A true lady will always remain faithful
to one perfume."

"Where'd you learn that?"

"Oh, everybody knows that. It's an old
French rule."

"But we aren't in France."

"Then why do you use French pefume?"

"Because they're the best."

"Of course, but if you follow one rule,

you've got to follow them all."

"Well, now, will you please inform me, Mr. Lee Anderson, just where you dug up all that twaddle?"

"Oh, I learned that during my formal education."

"What college did you go to?"

"None that you're acquainted with."

"Such as..."

"I studied in England and in Ireland, before coming back to the States."

"Why do you keep that job of yours? You could earn more money."

"I earn enough for what I want to do," I said.

"Tell me about your family."

"I had two brothers."

"And..."

"The younger died. In an accident."

"And the other."

"He's still living. He's in New York."

"I'd like to know him," she said.

She seemed to have lost the coldness she had displayed at Dexter's place and at Jicky's, and she also seemed to have forgotten what I'd done to her then.

"I'd rather you didn't know him," I said.

And I really meant it. I was wrong however, in thinking that she had forgotten :

"You've got a funny bunch of friends," she said, suddenly changing the subject.

We were still dancing since there was hardly any break between numbers. I avoided answering her.

"What did you do to Jean then," she asked. "She's completely changed."

"I didn't do anything to her. I just helped sober her up. In a special way I know."

"I can't make up my mind whether you're kidding me or not. It's hard to tell, with you."

"Oh, but I assure you I'm not hiding anything."

It was her turn not to say anything and for several minutes she just concentrated on dancing. She was completely relaxed in my arms, and didn't seem to be thinking about anything.

"I wish I had been there," she finally said.

"Too bad you weren't, " I said. "You'd be quite calm now."

Just saying that brought a warm flush behind my ears. I thought of Jean's body. Have both of them and then wipe them both out together, after having told them. That was too much to ask for.

"I don't think you really mean what you

say."

"I don't know what to say to make you believe I mean it."

She protested vigorously, called me a pedant and said I sounded like a Viennese psychiatrist. That was a bit too much.

"I mean," I explained, "just at what moments do you think I am telling the truth."

"I like it best when you say nothing."

"And when I do nothing too?"

I held her a bit closer to me. She must have realized what I meant, for she lowered her eyes. But I wasn't going to give up that easy. Besides, she said :

"That depends on just what you do."

"You don't approve of everything I do?"

"I don't think it's at all nice if you do it to everybody."

I thought I must be getting there. She was almost ripe. A little bit more effort. Yet I wanted to make sure.

"You're talking in riddles," I said. "Just what do you mean?"

She now lowered not only her eyes but her head as well. She was quite a lot smaller than I am. She had a big white carnation in her hair. She finally said:

"You know very well what I mean.

What you did to me, the other day, on the sofa."

"So..."

"Do you do that to all the women you meet?"

I laughed out loud until she pinched my arm.

"Don't make fun of me, I'm not a baby."

"Certainly not."

"Well answer me!"

"No," I said, "I don't do that to all the women. Frankly, there aren't too many women you feel like doing it to."

"You're joking again. After all, I could see the way your friends acted."

"They're not real friends, just chums."

"Don't quibble," she said. "Is that what you do then to all your... chums?"

"Do you really think I'd feel like doing that with girls like that?"

"I think..." she murmured, "that at certain times you can do all sorts of things with all sorts of people."

I decided I ought to take advantage of that statement to hold her even a bit tighter than before. At the same time, I tried to caress her breast. I had beat the gun the gun again. She broke out of my clasp slowly but firmly.

"You know, the other day, I had been

drinking," she stated.

"I don't believe it," I replied.

"Oh, - do you really think I would have let you do that if I hadn't been drinking?"

"Of course."

She lowered her head again, and then lifted it to say to me.

"You don't think I would have danced with just anybody?"

"I'm just anybody."

"You know very well you aren't."

I don't think I'd ever had such an up and down conversation. She slipped out of your fingers like an eel. For a moment you thought she'd go all the way, and then she'd suddenly back up at the least touch. I didn't give up though.

"What's so special about me?"

"I don't know. You're alright physically, but it isn't that. Your voice, maybe."

"Maybe what?"

"It isn't just an ordinary voice."

I again laughed heartily.

"No, she insisted, "It's a deeper voice, and more... I don't know just how to describe it... more serene, steady."

"That comes from singing and playing the guitar."

"No," she said, "I've never heard singers

or guitarists with a voice like yours. I have heard a voice that yours reminds me of, yes, it was back in Haiti. Some black men."

"Well, that's really a compliment." I said. "They're just about the best musicians you can find."

"Oh don't talk nonsense."

"It's not nonsense. They're the source of all American music," I said.

"I don't think so. All the big dance orchestras are whites."

"Of course-the whites are in a better position to exploit the Negro's inventions."

"I just don't think you're right."

"All the great popular composers are colored. Like Duke Ellington, for example."

"What about Gershwin, Kern, and all of those."

"They're all immigrants from Europe," I said: "They're the ones best able to envelop it. But I don't think you'd find a single original passage anywhere in Gershwin's work- one that hasn't been copied or plagiarized. Just try and find one in the Rhapsody in Blue, for example."

"You're funny,' she said. "I just hate the colored race."

That was just too wonderful. I thought of Tom, and I was almost ready to thank the

Lord. But I was too hot after that girl to be able to get mad at that moment. And I didn't need the Lord's help to do a good job.

"You're just like everybody else," I said. "You like to brag about things that everybody else but you discovered."

"I don't see just what you mean.'

"You ought to travel," I said. "You know, it wasn't just the white Americans all by themselves who invented the movies, the automobile, or nylon stockings, or horse-racing. Or jazz."

"Let's talk about something else," Lou said. "You read too much, I guess."

They were still at their bridge game on the table to a side, and I saw that I wouldn't get anywhere unless I made her drink something. I couldn't give up that easy.

"Dex told me about your rum," I went on. "Is it a myth, or can ordinary mortals have some?"

"Of course you can have some," Lou said. "I should have realized you'd be thirsty."

I let her go and she went off towards a sort of salon bar.

"Mix 'em?" she inquired. "White and caramel?"

"O.K., mix' em. Perhaps you could add some orange juice. I'm dying of thirst."

"Easy as pie," she said.

The bridge-players at the other end of the room cried out to us loudly.

"Hey, Lou! Make some for everybody."

"Alright," she said, "but you'll have to come and get it."

I just loved to watch her bend forward. She was wearing a sort of tight sweater which opened roundly in front, exposing part of her breasts, and her hair was now thrown to one side, as on the day I'd first seen her, but rather to the left. She had much less make-up on, and looked good enough to eat.

"You're a very beautiful girl," I said.

She straightened up, holding a bottle of rum in her hand.

"Please don't start in again."

"I'm not starting 'm continuing."

"Well then don't continue. You go much too fast. It's no fun that way."

"Things like that shouldn't last too long."

"Yes they should. Pleasant things should last forever."

"Do you know what really pleasant things are?"

"Yes. Talking to you, for example."

"But that's your pleasure. You're being selfish."

Boris Vian

"You're very nasty. Do you mean my conversation bores you?"

"I can't look at you without thinking that you are made for something very different than talking, and I can't talk to you without looking at you. But I'd just as well continue talking to you. That way I don't have to play bridge."

"You don't like bridge?"

She filled a glass and offered it to me. I took it and drank about half of it.

"Pretty good." I said appreciatively, looking at the glass. "And I like too the fact that you fixed it up for me."

She blushed.

"It's so nice, when you're like that."

"I assure you I can be nice in lots of other ways."

"But you have the wrong idea. You've got a good build physically and you think that that's all that any woman wants."

"Wants what?"

"Physical things."

"Those who don't want it," I asserted, "have never tried it."

"That isn't true."

"Have you ever tried?"

She didn't answer, but just wrung her fingers, and then she made up her mind.

"What you did to me, last time..."

"Yes..."

"It wasn't very pleasant. It was... it was terrible."

"But,... it wasn't unpleasant, was it?"

"No..." she said in barely a whisper.

I didn't press my point, but just finished my drink. I'd recovered the ground I'd lost. God, what a tough time I'd have with this girl. Some fish really do put up a battle.

Jean had gotten up and came over to get the drinks.

"Do you find Lou too boring?"

"How nice you are!" said her sister.

"Lou is very charming," I said. "I like her very much. May I have the honor of asking you for her hand."

"Not while I'm alive," said Jean. "I come first."

"And what does that make me," said Lou, "an orphan?"

"You're too young," said Jean. "You've still got plenty of time. As for me..."

I laughed, since Jean hardly looked more than a couple of years older than her sister.

"Don't laugh like a big dope," Lou said. "Don't you think she looks old and withered?"

I definitely liked both of them. And they seemed to understand each other too.

"If you don't look any worse than her when you get older," I said to Lou, "I'd be glad to marry both of you."

"You're just terrible," Jean said. "I'm going back and play bridge. You'll dance with me soon, won't you?"

"No, you won't," Lou said. "This time I'm first. Go play your nasty old cards."

We danced again for a while, but the program changed and I suggested to Lou that we take a stroll outside.

"I don't think I really want to be left alone with you," she said.

"There's nothing for you to worry about. After all, all you'd have to do is holler."

"Oh, yeah!" she objected, "and make everybody think I'm a big baby."

"Alright," I said. "In that case how about going for a drink, if you don't mind."

I went over to the bar and mixed myself a little stimulant. Lou remained where I left her.

"Like some?"

She shook her head no, closing her yellow eyes. I decided to leave her alone and I crossed the room to watch Jean's game.

"Bring you luck," I said.

"About time, too!"

She turned easily towards me with a radiant smile.

"I'm losing about a hundred and thirty dollars. Not so nice, is it?"

"That depends on how many millions you've got left," I said.

"Shall we stop now?" she suggested. The other three players didn't seem to be especially enthusiastic about continuing, and the game broke up. As for Dexter, he'd long since taken the other girl into the garden.

"Is that all you can get?" Jean asked, pointing to the radio with a grimace of displeasure. "I'm going to try to find something else."

She turned the knobs around until she got something that could be danced to. One of the two fellows invited Lou. The other couple danced. I took Jean for a drink before we started. I knew what she needed.

XIII

When Dex and I went up to go to bed, I'd hardly said another word to Lou after our long conversation. Our rooms were on the first floor, on the same side as the girls'. The girls' parents had rooms in the other wing. The local characters had gone home. As a matter of fact the girls' parents weren't in the other wing at all, but were in New York or in Haiti or some place like that. My room was at one end, then Dex's, then Jean's, and finally Lou's. I wasn't in exactly the best spot for my purposes.

I got undressed, took a nice shower and then rubbed myself all over with a rough towel. I heard Dexter moving around in his room. He went out and then came back a couple of minutes later, and I then heard the sound of somebody taking a drink. He must have made a little trip down to the liquor supply and I thought it wasn't a bad idea at all. I knocked lightly on the door between his bedroom and the bathroom. He came over right away.

"Say! Dex," I said through the door. "Am I dreaming or did I hear some bottles clinking?"

"How about having one," said Dex. "I brought up a pair of them."

It was a bottle of rum. Nothing better to help you fall asleep, or to keep you awake, depending on who, when and where. I expected to keep awake, but I heard Dex go to bed pretty soon after. It affected him differently from me.

I waited a half hour and then slipped quietly out of my room. I had one pair of shorts and my pajama tops. I can't stand wearing pajama bottoms. They drive me wild.

It was dark in the corridor, but I knew where I was going. I walked forward none too cautiously, since the rug was thick enough to muffle the noise of a ball-game, and I rapped softly on Lou's door.

I heard her come over. Or rather I felt her come, and then the catch turned. I slipped into her room and softly closed the paneled door.

She had on a stunning white dressing-gown which she must have stolen from a Varga girl. I could also see that she had on a lacy brassiere and a set of panties to match.

"I came to see if you're still mad at me," I said.

"You can't stay here," she objected.

"Why did you answer the door then?

Who did you think it was?"

"I don't know, - Susie I guess."

"Susie's sleeping. And so are all the
other servants. You know that as well as I do."

"Just what do you want?"

"Just this."

I caught her in my arms and kissed her
with all I had. I have no idea what my left
hand was doing then. But she fought back and
I caught on my left ear one of the best socks
I've ever caught in my time. I let her go.

"You're a brute," she said.

Her hair was done up in the usual way,
loosely, and parted in the center, and she
looked just delicious. I kept myself calm, however. The rum helped me.

"You're making too much noise," I
answered. "Jean'll hear you."

"There's a bathroom between our two
rooms."

"Oh! Fine!"

I went at her again and opened up her
night-gown. I managed to tear at her panties
before she could hit me again. Then I caught
her wrist and held her hands behind her back.
She rested easily in the hollow of my right
palm. She fought without a sound but with all
her anger. She tried to butt me with her knees,
but I slipped my left hand around the small of

her back and pressed her tight against me. She tried to bite me through my pajamas. I couldn't get my damn shorts off. I suddenly let her go and pushed her towards her bed.

"Well," I said, "you've put on a pretty good show, but I'll be damned if I'm going to wear myself out for nothing at all."

She looked as though she were going to cry, but her eyes shone with anger too. She didn't even try to cover herself, and I got an eyeful. She had a thick black muff, shiny like astrakhan fur.

I just turned my back to her and went to the door.

"Sleep well," I said. "Pardon me for the slight damage I've done to your underwear. I don't dare suggest that I buy you a new set, but I assure you will send me the bill."

I couldn't have cut her any harder, though I've got to admit I've got some talent in that respect. She didn't say a thing, but I saw her clench her fists and she bit her lips. She turned her back on me suddenly, and I paused for an instant to admire her. It was really a shame. I went out feeling very funny.

But not enough to bother me when I went into the next room, Jean's. She hadn't locked the door. I calmly went to the bathroom door and turned the bolt.

And then I took off my pajama top and dropped my shorts. The room was lit by the soft light of a floor lamp and deep orange drapes helped give a soft tone to the room. Jean was stretched out on her tummy on her low bed, quite nude, and was doing her nails. She turned her head when she saw me come in and followed me with her eyes as I locked the door.

"You've got a lot of nerve!" she said.

"Uh-huh,' I said. "And you, you were waiting for me."

She laughed and rolled over on her bed. I sat down next to her and caressed her thighs. She had about as much notion of modesty as a day old baby. She sat up and felt my biceps.

"Gee, you're strong!"

"I'm as weak as a new-born lamb," I replied.

She rubbed herself against me and kissed me, and then she suddenly twisted back and wiped her lips.

"You've just been with Lou. I can smell perfume on you.."

I hadn't even thought of that damn give-away. Jean's voice was unsteady, and she turned her eyes away from mine. I took her firmly by the shoulders.

"Be reasonable!"

"I can smell her perfume on you."

"I went to her to apologize," I said. "I'd been annoying her downstairs."

I thought of Lou who must have still been there in her room, almost altogether nude, and the thought of it excited me even more. Jean noticed it and blushed.

"Does that bother you," I asked her.

"No-o," she murmured. "Can I touch you?"

I stretched myself out alongside her and made her get down too. She slid her hands timidly over my body.

"You're very strong," she said softly.

We were now on our sides, facing each other. I pressed softly on her body and rolled her over and then snuggled up against her.

She spread her legs a bit to let me in.

"You're going to hurt me," she said.

"Of course not," I said.

I did nothing more than run my fingers over her breasts, cupping them and then coming up to the nipples, and I felt her tremble against my body. Her warm round buttocks fitted tightly into my thighs and she was breathing hard.

"Should I put out the light?" I murmured.

"No," Jean said, "I like it better this

way."

I drew my left hand out from under her body and brushed her hair away from her right ear. Many men don't know what you can do to a woman by kissing and nibbling at her ear-it works wonders. Jean twisted about like an eel.

"Don't do that!"

I stopped at once, but she grabbed my wrist and pressed hard up against me.

"Do it again."

I did it again for a longer time, and I felt her suddenly stiffen and then relax. Her head fell to the mattress. My hand slid along her belly and I could see that she had really felt something. I began to run my lips over her neck, yet hardly touching it with my kisses. I could see her flesh tense as I moved toward her throat. And then, very slowly, I took my penis and put it into her, so easily that I don't think she even knew it until I began to move it about. It all depends on how you build them up. She suddenly jerked herself away.

"Am I hurting you?" I asked.

"No, but caress me some more. Caress me all night long."

"That's just what I'm going to do," I said.

I took her again, this time roughly. But I

stopped before she was satisfied.

"You'll drive me crazy," she murmured.

She rolled over on her belly, hiding her head in her arms. I kissed her back and her buttocks, and then I got on my knees on top of her.

"Spread your legs," I said.

She didn't say anything but spread her legs slowly. I slipped my hand in between her thighs and I again directed my penis, but I hit the wrong spot. She stiffened again, but I insisted.

"I don't want to," she said.

"Get on your knees."

"I don't want to."

But she arched her back and pulled her knees forward. She still had her head hidden by her arms, and, very slowly, I did what I wanted to do. She again didn't say anything, but I could feel her stomach rise and fall and her breath quicken. I dropped on my side without withdrawing from her, pulling her with me, and when I tried to see her face I saw that there were tears under her closed eyes, but she told me not to withdraw.

XIV

About five o'clock in the morning I went back to my room. Jean hadn't moved since I'd let go my embrace-she was thoroughly worn out. I felt a bit weak in the knees, but I managed to get up from my bed about ten o'clock. I think the rum that Dex gave me did me a lot of good. I got under the cold shower and then asked him to box with me a while. He hit like a mule, and that put me back on my mettle. I thought of how Jean must feel. Dex had had to much rum; his breath knocked you down from the other end of the room. I told him to sop up a lot of tomato juice and then do a round of golf. He thought he was going to play the promised set of tennis with Jean, but she hadn't gotten up. I went down for breakfast. Lou was sitting at the table, all alone. She was wearing a pleated skirt and a light silk blouse under a deerskin jacket. I really felt something for her. But after that night I was fairly calm. I said good morning.

"Good morning."

Her tone was quite cold. Perhaps rather sad.

"Are you mad at me? May I apologize for last night?"

"I suppose you can't help it," she said, "you were born that way."

"No, I grew up that way."

"I don't think that's funny."

"I guess you're too young to be interested."

"You'll be sorry you said that to me, Lee."

"I'd like to see the day."

"Let's not talk anymore about it. Would you like to play a set with me."

"Glad to," I said, "I could use a bit of relaxation."

She couldn't help smiling, and as soon as we'd finished breakfast, I followed her to the court. She wasn't the kind to bear a grudge.

We played until about noon. I could hardly stand up and was beginning to see everything in a haze. Just then Jean came up and Dex too. They looked to be in as bad shape as I was.

"Hi!" I said to Jean. "You look in rare form."

"Take a look at yourself," she cried back.

"It's Lou's fault," I said.

"I suppose it's my fault too if Dex looks as though he's got a foot in the grave too!" Lou said indignantly. "You just had too much rum, and that's what you get. Oh, Dex! I can smell you a mile away!"

"Lee only said half a mile," Dex objected strenuously.

"Did I say that?"

"Lou," Dex said, "Come play a game with me."

"That isn't fair," Lou cried, "You're supposed to play with Jean."

"No, sir!" Jean cried out. "Come on, Lee, take me for a ride before breakfast."

"Jesus Christ, what time do you eat breakfast around here?" Dex said with feigned surprise.

"Any old time," said Jean seriously.

She put her arm through mine and led me towards the garage.

"Should we take Dex's car?" I asked. "It's right in back and the easiest to get out."

She didn't answer. She held my arm very tightly and snuggled up against me as close as possible. I made myself say some insignificant things, and she still didn't say anything. She let me go to get in the car, but as soon as I got in she snuggled up against me again, as close as she could without making it impossible for me to drive. I backed out and raced down the driveway. The gate was open and I turned right. I didn't know where that would take us.

"How do you get out of this town?" I
asked Jean.

"Any old way," she murmured.

I looked at her in the mirror. Her
eyes were closed.

"Say, you know," I said, "you must have
slept too much and it's made you very dull."

She suddenly straightened up and took
my head hard in her two hands and kissed me.
I braked quickly-I wasn't exactly in a position
to watch the road.

"Kiss me, Lee."

"Wait at least until we get out of town."

"Oh, I don't care what people will say. I
don't care if they all know about it."

"And your reputation?"

"Don't worry about it, just kiss me!"

Well I don't mind kissing for about five
minutes or so, but I don't feel like doing just
that all the time. Lay her and go all over her,
that's something. But not just kissing. I broke
loose.

"Be reasonable."

"Kiss me, Lee. Please..."

I stepped on the gas again and
took a sharp turn to the right at the first corner,
and then to the left : I tried to shake her off
somehow so she'd let me go and hold onto

something else, but it was no go with that car :
it rode too damn smoothly. All she did was
put her arms more tightly about my neck.

"But people'll talk about you."

"I wish they would talk. They'll be so
embarrassed later."

"When they know we're going to get
married."

Glory, but she had sure developed fast.
Some of them are affected by it like cats by cat-
nip, or dogs by a dead frog. They just never
want to let go.

"We're going to get married?"

She leaned down and kissed my right
hand.

"Of course."

"When?"

"Right now."

"But not on Sunday."

"Why not"? she asked.

"No. It's silly. Your father and mother
won't like it."

"I don't care."

"I haven't got any money."

"Enough for the two of us."

"Hardly enough for myself," I said.

"My father will give us some."

"I don't think so. Your father and mother don't know me. And you don't know me

either, for that matter."

She blushed and hid her head on my shoulder.

"Yes, I do know you," she murmured. "I could describe every inch of you with my eyes closed."

I wanted to see just how bad she was hooked so I said :

"Lots of women could describe me like that."

She didn't look shocked.

"I don't care. They won't do it any more."

"But you don't know anything about me."

"I didn't know about you..."

And she started to hum the popular song that goes that way.

"And you don't know anything more now," I told her.

"So tell me, then." she said.

"Well," I said, "I don't see how I could stop you from marrying me. Unless I go away. And I don't feel like doing that."

I didn't say "before having laid Lou too" but that is what I thought. Jean was all gone on me. I had her in the palm of my hand. I now had to speed up my campaign with Lou. Jean put her head on my knees and curled up on the car seat.

"Please tell me about yourself, Lee."

"O.K." I said.

I told her that I was born somewhere in California, that my father was of Swedish descent and that was where I'd gotten my blond hair. I had had a hard time as a kid because my parents were very poor, and when I was about nine years old during the depression I started playing the guitar to earn some money and then when I was fourteen I had the good luck to meet a fellow that got interested in me and took me to Europe with him, to England and Ireland where I stayed almost ten years.

That was a pretty good fairy tale. I did spend almost ten years in Europe, but not under circumstances like that. And everything I had learned I owed just to myself and to the library in the place I'd worked in as a servant. I didn't tell her either just how the master there treated me-he knew I was colored-nor about what he did to me when his little friends didn't happen to show up. Nor about how I left him, after making him sign a check to pay my return passage, in return for certain special personal services.

I invented a big heap of lies about my brother Tom, and about the kid, and how he had died in an accident, — it was caused by some niggers, I said, they're a sly bunch, good only to be servants, and she said she couldn't stand having them near her. Well when I came back I found that my parents home had been sold, and my brother Tom was now in New York, and my kid brother six foot under. I then decided to look for work, and I owed my present job to a friend of Tom's. That bit was true.

She listened to me attentively as though it were the Gospel truth, so I pilled on some more. I told her that I thought her parents wouldn't let us get married, since she wasn't old enough. She said she was just twenty, and in that state that was old enough to get married without the parents permission. But I didn't earn enough money. She said she'd rather have me earn my own money honestly, and then her parents would surely like me and find me an important job in Haiti or on one of their plantations. While we were talking I tried to get myself located, and I finally hit on the road Dex and I had taken when we came there. I said I'd go back to my work in the meantime, and she'd come and see me sometime during the week. We'd fix things up to go away somewhere to the southwest where we could be together a couple of days someplace where nobody'd bother us, and then when we came back married, it'd be too late for anybody to do anything about it.

I asked her if she'd tell Lou. She said she would, but not what we'd done together. Just talking about it got her excited again. I was glad we got back.

XV

We spent the afternoon just any old way. It wasn't as nice as the day before. Real autumn weather. I took care not to get caught in a bridge game with the girls' local friends. I remembered Dex's advice and realized it wasn't the time to risk throwing away the couple of hundred dollars I'd managed to save up. It's true that those people didn't give a rap when they lost five or six hundred a throw. All they were interested in was killing time.

Jean just kept looking at me all the time, and I whispered to her when nobody was looking to be more careful. I still danced with Lou, but she didn't trust me. I couldn't get her to talk about anything interesting. I'd gotten back the strength I'd knocked out of myself the night before, and I began to get excited everytime I looked at her breasts. As a matter of fact she didn't offer any objections when I petted her a little while dancing. Like the night before, the local people left fairly early, leaving the four of us. Jean could hardly keep on her feet, but she still wanted to go at it. I had a tough time persuading her to wait a while. Fortunately her tiredness kept her down. Dex kept on guzzling lots of rum. We went up about ten o'clock, and I went down again right after to get a book. I didn't feel like going at it again with Jean, and I wasn't sleepy enough to go to bed right away.

And then, when I got back to my room, I found Lou sitting on my bed. She had on the same nightgown as the night before, but different panties. I didn't touch her. I locked my door and also the door to the bathroom, and I lay down without even looking at her. I heard her breath come quickly while I was taking off my clothes. After I got in bed, I decided to talk to her.

"Not sleepy tonight, Lou? Can I do something for you?"

"I'm just making sure you don't go to Jean's room tonight," she said.

"Where'd you get the idea I went there last night?"

"I heard you," she said.

"That's funny. I don't think I made any noise," I said mockingly.

"Why did you lock the doors?"

"I always lock the doors when I go to sleep," I said. "I don't want to wake up and find anybody lying next to me."

She must have put perfume on every square inch of her skin. You could have smelt her miles away. Her make up was just right too. She had her hair done up like the night before and all I'd have to do to pluck her like a ripe plum was stretch out my hand. However, I had an account to straighten out with her first.

"You were in Jean's room," she repeated.

"Well all I can remember is that you kicked me out," I replied.

"I don't think much of your manners at all," she said.

"I don't see that there was anything wrong with them tonight," I said. "I apologize for having undressed before you, but I'm sure you didn't look, so that's alright."

"Just what did you do to Jean?" she wanted to know.

"Listen," I said. "I am going to give you a big surprise and tell you the exact truth. I think you should know. I kissed her the other day, and ever since then she won't let me alone."

"When?"

"The time I sobered her up at Jicky's house."

"I knew it!"

"She almost forced me to. You know I was a little drunk myself."

"Did you really kiss her...?"

"What do you mean, really?"

"Like you did me," she murmured.

"No," I said with a tone of frankness that I felt very proud of. "Your sister gets on my nerves. You're the one I really want, Lou. I kissed Jean the way…, well, the way I'd kiss my mother, and she got the wrong idea. I don't know how I can get her off of me now — I'm afraid I just won't be able to. She'll probably tell you we're going to get married. She got that idea in her head this morning in Dex's car. She's pretty, alright, but I just don't go for her. I think she's a little silly myself."

"But I saw you kiss her since."

"She was the one who kissed me. You know that if you take care of somebody that's drunk, he'll always be grateful to you."

"Are you sorry you kissed her?"

"No," I said, "There's only one thing I'm sorry and that's the fact that it wasn't you that was drunk instead of her."

"You can kiss me now," she said.

She didn't move but, just looked straight in front of her. It must have required quite an effort of will for her to say that.

"I can't kiss you, Lou," I said. "With Jean it didn't matter very much. But with you it's different. I don't want to touch you until…"

I didn't finish and, uttering a discour-

aged sigh, I turned over on my side with my
back to her.

"Until what?" Lou asked.

She had spun around and put her hand
on my arm.

"It's crazy," I said. "It just impossible."

"Tell me."

"I meant... until we were married. You
and me, Lou. But you're too young, and
besides I could never be free of Jean,—she'd
never let us alone."

"Do you seriously mean you'd do that."

"Do what?'

"Marry me?"

"I can't say I'm serious about something
that just couldn't be,' I replied. "But if you
mean, is that what I really want and desire, I
swear that I am."

She got up from the bed. I lay there
with my back to her. She didn't say a word. I
didn't either, and then I felt her lie down on
the bed.

"Lee," she said after a while.

My heart was beating so strongly I
thought I heard it pound on the bed. I turned
around. She'd taken off her dressing-gown
and everything else and was lying on her back
with her eyes closed. I think Howard Hughes
would have been inspired to a dozen pictures

if he had seen her breasts. I didn't touch her.

"I don't want to with you," I said.
"I find this business about Jean just disgusting.
Before you met me, you two got along swell
together. I don't want to be coming between
you."

The way I felt then I didn't want to do
anything but screw her until the cows came
home, but I managed to control myself.

"Jean is in love with you," Lou said.
"You can't help notice it."

"I can't do anything about it."

She was as smooth and slender as a
blade of grass, and as fragrant as a perfume-
shop. I sat down and bent over her and kissed
her between her thighs on the little ridges
where a woman's flesh is as soft as eider-
down. She drew her legs together, but spread
them again almost at once, and I again bent
down, but a bit higher this time. Her shiny,
curly muff caressed my cheek and I began to
lick it tenderly. Her vagina was hot and moist,
the lips thick under my tongue,—I wanted
very much to bite it, but I straightened up. She
got up suddenly and grasped my head to put
it back. I tried to release myself.

"I don't want to," I said. "I just don't
want to as long as I 'm not sure I'm free of Jean.
I can't marry both of you."

I nibbled at her nipples. She still held my head and kept her eyes closed.

"Jean wants to marry me," I continued. "But why should she? And if I say no, she'll surely fix things up so that we won't be able to see each other."

She arched her back in response to my caresses, and didn't reply. My right hand ran up and down her thighs. She opened them swiftly each time I touched the right spot.

"There's only one way to get out of it," I said. "I can marry Jean and you'll come along with us, and we'll manage to get together."

"I don't want to that," Lou murmured.

Her voice rose and fell unevenly. I felt I could have played it like a musical instrument. She changed in tone as I touched her differently.

"I don't want you to do that to her."

"There's nothing to oblige me to do it to her," I said.

"Oh, do it to me," Lou cried. "Do it right away."

She trembled, and each time that my hand rose she withered in response. I slipped my head in between her legs, and then turned her over with her back to me. I lifted her leg and moved my mouth in between her thighs and I took her vagina in my lips. She suddenly stiffened and then relaxed immediately. I sucked for a moment and then withdrew. She was lying flat on her face.

"Lou," I murmured. "I don't want to screw you. I just don't want to screw you until we can feel sure of ourselves. I'm going to marry Jean and then we'll manage. You'll help me."

She rolled over on her back quickly and kissed me in a sort of furor. Her teeth struck mine and with my hands I caressed her back. And then I took her by the waist and stood her up.

"Go back to bed," I said to her. "We've said a lot of silly things. Be a good girl and go back to bed."

I got up too and kissed her eyes. I was glad I'd kept my jockey shorts on under my pajama tops and could preserve my dignity.

I put her bra and panties back on and I wiped her thighs with the sheet and then I put on her negligee. She let me do as I pleased in silence. She was soft and warm in my arms.

"To bed, my dear," I said. "I'm going away tomorrow. Try to be up for breakfast, I'd like to see you again then."

And then I let her outside and closed the door again. I now felt that I had both of them hooked. I felt very good inside of me and I'm sure my kid brother was happy in his grave. I stretched out my hand to him. It's nice to be able to shake your brother's hand.

XVI

I got a letter from Tom a couple of day later. He didn't tell me much about what he was doing. I deduced that he'd found a not to wonderful job in a school in Harlem, and he cited a passage from the Scriptures, giving me the exact chapter and verse, because he knew I wasn't very well up on that stuff. It was a passage from the book of Job, 13:14, which said : "Wherefore do I take my flesh in my teeth, and put my life in mine hand."

I guess the way Tom interpreted it, it meant that he was playing his trump card, shooting the works for big stakes, and I thought it was a pretty involved way of saying something as simple as that. I could see that Tom hadn't changed much in that respect. But he was a god guy anyhow. I wrote him and told him that everything was fine with me, and I put in a money order for fifty bucks, because I suspected he wasn't eating too well.

As for the rest, there wasn't much to tell. Books and more books. I got some special Christmas stuff and also some offers from other outfits not hooked up with our company, from salesmen working on their own account. My contract forbade any such purchases and I didn't feel like jeopardizing my position that way. At times I had to kick out some other characters, specialists in pornography. I wasn't too harsh with them however : they were often colored men of all shades and I knew they didn't have too easy a time of it. I usually took one or two items from them and gave them to the bunch. Judy in particular liked such stuff.

They still hung around in the drug-store and came to see me, and I still laid the girls regularly, every other day for the most part. They were just dumb rather than vicious. Except for Judy.

Both Jean and Lou were going to come through Buckton sometime during the week. I made dates with both of them. Then I got a call from Jean and found out that Lou couldn't come. Then Jean wanted to invite me up to their place for the weekend instead, but I told her I couldn't come. I wasn't going to let myself be ordered around by her like a hired hand. She said that made her very sorry and she really wanted me to come, but I told her I had a lot of work to catch up on. She then promised to come on Monday around five o'clock. That way we'd have plenty of time to talk.

I didn't do anything special till next

Monday. Saturday night I took the place of the
guitarist at the Stork Club. I got fifteen bucks
for the night, and drinks on the house, which
wasn't bad for that town. At home I read or
practiced on the guitar. I'd more or less
dropped tap-dancing—I was popular enough
without that. I thought I'd go back to that a
little after I'd gotten rid of the Asquith girls. I
bought myself some bullets for the kid's little
gun, and I also got an assortment of drugs. I
took my car to the garage for a checkup and
the mechanic took care of some things that
weren't in A1 condition.

There wasn't a sign of life from Dex all
this time. I 'd tried to see him Saturday morning, but he'd just left for the weekend, they
didn't know just where. I guessed that he'd
been back with his ten year old kids at Anna's
place, because the rest of the bunch didn't
know where he'd been all week either.

Monday, about twenty after four, Jean's
car pulled up outside the door. She didn't give
a hang what people might say. She got out
and came into the store. We were alone. She
came over to me and gave me a kiss she must
have been saving up for a long time, and I
asked her to sit down. I purposely didn't close
the venetian blinds so she could see I didn't
like her coming ahead of time. She didn't look

good in spite of her make up, and she had
black circles under her eyes. As usual she was
dressed in the very latest and most expensive
clothes—her hat very definitely didn't come
from Macy's ground floor. It made her look
somewhat older, incidentally.

"Have a nice ride?" I asked her.

"It's very close," she answered. "I'd
thought it was farther away."

"You're early," I remarked.

"She looked at her diamond-studded
watch.

"Not very. It's twenty-five to."

"Twenty-nine after four," I corrected.
"You're fast."

"Are you sorry?"

She'd adopted a coy manner that got on
my nerves.

"Of course. I've got other things to do
besides fool around."

"Lee," she murmured, "Be nice."

"I'm nice when I haven't got any work
to do."

"Be nice, Lee," she said again. "I'm
going to have... I'm..."

She paused. I knew what she was
going to say but I wanted her to
say it.

"What do you mean?" I said.

"I'm going to have a baby, Lee."

"You've been letting some man take advantage of you," I said, wagging my finger at her.

She laughed, but her face remained drawn and tense.

"Lee, you've got to marry me right away, otherwise there'll be a terrible scandal."

"Of course not," I said. "Things like that happen every day."

I had now assumed a bantering air. Still I didn't want her to run off before I'd arranged everything. Never can tell what a woman in her condition would do. I went over to her and stroked her shoulders.

"Sit there a minute," I said. "I'll lock up the store and then we'll be more at ease."

Now that she was going to have a baby it oughtn't be too hard to get rid of her. She now had a good reason for wanting to kill herself. I locked the door and went over the window to draw the venetian blinds to screen us. I let them down easy with only a slight screeching sound as the rope pulled through.

When I came back to her, Jean had taken off her hat, and was stroking her hair to bring back its glossiness. She looked lot better that way, a real pretty girl in any language.

"When are we going to leave?" she
asked suddenly. "You've got to take me away
as soon as possible."

"We could go towards the end of this
week. My business here is in good order. But
I'd have to find another job down there."

"I'll take along enough money."

I certainly didn't intend to let myself be
supported, even by a girl I expected to kill.

"That makes no difference to me," I said.
"I can never take your money. Let's have that
understood once and for all."

She didn't answer. She squirmed
in her seat as though she was afraid to say
something.

"Go ahead,' I said to encourage her.
"Spill it. What've you done without telling
me?"

"I wrote down there," she said. "I saw
an address in the ads, they said it's a rather
deserted place, for people who like to be alone,
for newlyweds who want to have privacy for
their honeymoon."

"If all the newlyweds who want to be
alone went down there," I muttered, "It ought
to look like Union Station."

She laughed. She looked relieved. She
wasn't the kind that could keep a secret.

"They answered my letter," she said.

"We'll have a separate cabin to sleep in, and we'll eat at the hotel itself."

"The best thing you could do is to go as soon as you can, and I'll come later. That way I'll be able to finish everything."

"I'd rather go with you."

"Can't do it. You better go home and don't pack your things till the last minute so as not to arouse suspicion. You won't have to take many things along. And don't leave any note telling where you're going. Your parents don't have to know."

"When will you come?"

"Next Monday. I'll leave Sunday night."

If I left Sunday night it wouldn't be noticed. But I still had to arrange about Lou.

"Of course," I added, "you've told your sister about it."

"Not yet."

"She must suspect something. Anyhow I think it's a good idea to let her know. She can act as go-between. You understand each other, don't you?"

"Yes."

"Then tell her, but not till the day you leave. Leave her your address, but in such a way that she won't know until after you've gone."

"How can I do that?"

"You can put it in an envelope and mail it after you're a couple of hundred miles away from home. Or you can leave it in her room. There are lots of ways."

"I don't like all these complications. Oh, Lee, can't we just go away, the two of us, telling everybody that we just want to be alone."

"I can't do that," I said. "Maybe you can, but I haven't got any money."

"It makes no difference to me."

"Take a look at yourself," I said. "You can say that now because you have money."

"I don't dare tell Lou about it. She's only fifteen."

I laughed.

"Do you think she's just a baby in diapers? You ought to know that in a family where there are several sisters, the youngest learns everything at about the same time as the oldest. If you had a little sister ten years old, she'd know as much as Lou."

"But Lou is just a kid."

"Sure, sure. All you've got to see is the way she dresses. And the perfumes she uses show how innocent she is. I say you've got to tell Lou. You've got to have somebody to be able to keep in touch with your parents indirectly."

"I'd rather nobody knew about it."

I laughed sarcastically.

"You're not so proud of the guy you hooked, eh?"

Her mouth began to tremble and I thought she was going to cry. She got up.

"Why are you so mean to me? Does it give you pleasure to hurt me? I don't want anybody to know because I'm afraid."

"Afraid of what?"

"Afraid you'd leave me before we got married."

I shrugged.

"Do you think being married would stop me if I wanted to leave you."

"If we had a baby it would."

"If we had a baby I wouldn't be able to get a divorce so easy, that's all. But that wouldn't stop me from leaving you if I felt that way."

She finally broke into tears. She fell back into her chair and lowered her head, and the tears rolled down her cheeks. I saw that I was going a bit too fast, so I went over to her. I put my hand on the back of her neck and caressed it softly.

"Oh, Lee!" she cried, "Everything is so different from what I expected it to be. I thought you'd be happy to have me all for yourself."

I said something silly, and then she began to vomit. I didn't have anything around and I had to run to the back room to get a rag that the cleaning woman used to dust the place with. I wondered if it was the baby that made her sick. When she'd stopped heaving, I wiped her face with her handkerchief. Her eyes were clear and shiny with tears, and she breathed with difficulty. She'd gotten her shoes dirty, and I wiped them with a piece of paper. The smell bothered me, but I bent over her and kissed her. She crushed me to her and poured out a torrent of words of endearment. I had never had any luck with her. Always sick, either from having drunk too much or screwed too much.

"You'd better leave," I said. "Go home. Take care of yourself. Then, get your things together and take off. I'll come to you next Monday. I've already got the ring."

This surprise cheered her up again, and she smiled incredulously.

"Lee, do you mean it?"

"Of course I do."

"Oh, Lee, I'm crazy about you. I know we're going to be very happy."

She didn't have a trace of bitterness. Most girls aren't that easy. I stood her up and caressed her breasts through her dress. She became tense and arched herself. She wanted me to keep it up. I wanted to air out the place, but she held me tight and with one hand unbuttoned my pants. I lifted her dress and put her on the long counter where my customers left the books they'd looked at. She closed her eyes and looked dead. When I felt her relax I kept it up until she began to moan. I went off on her dress, and then she sat up suddenly lifting her hand to her mouth, and vomited again.

And then I put her on her feet again and buttoned her coat. I carried her almost up to her car, going through the store's side entrance and I set her down behind the wheel. She looked deathly sick, but she still had strength enough to bite my lower lip till the blood came. I didn't complain. I then watched her drive off. I think her car knew the road, and it was lucky for her.

Right after that I went upstairs to my room and took a bath to get rid of the smell.

XVII

Until that minute I hadn't thought of all the complications my plan to kill both of the girls would bring about. For a moment I felt like dropping the whole business and go on just selling my books and earning a good living. But I had to do something for the kid, and for Tom, and for my own sake too. I know some men more or less like me who try to forget their blood and who go over to the side of the whites for all purposes, not even having the decency to refrain from knocking the colored race when the occasion demands it. I could kill men like that with a lot of pleasure, but I had to do things in the proper order.

First the Asquith girls. I'd had plenty of chances to knock off the others : the kids I fooled around with, Judy, Jicky, Bill and Betty, but they didn't interest me too much. They weren't important enough. The Asquiths would be my first test-case. Then after I'd gotten that over with, I thought I'd go after something really big. Maybe a senator, or something like that. I'd have to have plenty to keep myself calm. But I had to think things over a little about how I'd get away with it, once I had those two dead females on my hands.

The best thing to do would be to make it look like an auto accident. People would wonder what they were doing all the way down there near the border, but they'd stop wondering after the autopsy, when they'd find out that Jean was pregnant. Lou they'd figure, had just gone along with her sister. And me, I wouldn't be anywhere around. Except that when the whole business was over, I expected to let their parents in on it. They'd know that their darling daughter had got it from a "nigger." Then I would have to find a new stamping grounds and start in all over again. A crazy plan, but the craziest are the ones that usually work out. I was sure that Lou could be made to come down there with us. I had a lot of power over her. Then an auto ride with her sister. Jean driving, and then a fainting-spell. What could be more natural? I'd have plenty of time to jump out. I shouldn't have any trouble finding a spot where it would work out in the kind of country we were going to. Lou'd be up front with her sister, and me in back. Lou first, and if Jean saw it and let go the wheel, that's all I'd need.

Except that I wasn't too enthusiastic about this auto business. First of all, it's an old gag. And besides, it would be too quick. I wanted to have time to tell them why, and I wanted them to know I had them, to know in advance what was coming to them.

The auto...I'd leave that for later, to finish up with. I thought I had it. First take them to a quiet spot. There give them the dope, and then let them have it. Then put them back in the car and stage the accident. Just as easy and a lot more satisfactory to me. I wondered if it would be so easy.

I still thought a lot about it. I began to get nervous. Once I was going to throw the whole business out the window and decided it wouldn't come off the way I expected it to, and then I remembered the kid. And I remebered my last conversation with Lou. I'd begun to prepare the ground with her, and that made it more definite. It was worth running the risk. If I could, I'd use the car. If not, so what. The border wouldn't be too far away and they don't kill you for that in Mexico. I think I must have had that plan in my head all the time, more or less vaguely, and I was just now beginning to realize what I wanted to work out.

I drank a lot of whiskey those days. My brain was in a fury. I got some other tools besides the bullets. I bought a pick and a shovel and some rope. I still didn't know I'd be able to work it out the way I'd just figured it. If yes I'd need the bullets. If no, then the other things would be useful. Then too, the pick and shovel gave me a sense of security with respect to another little idea that had crossed my mind. I think that anybody who intends to commit a crime is wrong if he figures out all the details in advance. I think you've always got to trust to luck. But you've got to have the necessary tools on hand when luck strikes. I don't know if I was wrong not to figure it out exactly, but when I thought over all I'd heard about such auto accidents, the idea appealed to me less and less. I hadn't considered one important factor : that of time. I'd have plenty of time and didn't worry too much about that. Nobody'd know where we were going and I thought Lou wouldn't tell anybody, if our last conversation had had any effect on her. I'd know that as soon as I got there.

And then, at the very last minute, about an hour before I was about to start, a sort of fright came over me, and I began to wonder if I'd find Lou when I got there. That was the most horrible moment I've ever lived through. I sat at the table and drank. I don't know how many drinks, but my brain remained as clear as though Ricardo's stuff had been changed into rainwater. I also saw very clearly just what I had to do, as clearly as I'd seen Tom's face when the gas-can had blown up in the kitchen. I went down to the drug-store and got in to the phone booth. I dialed the operator and asked for long distance and then for Prixville and got through right away. The chamber-maid told me Lou would be there in a second, - there she was.

"Hello," she said.

"This is Lee Anderson. How are you?"

"What's the matter?"

"Jean gone away, hasn't she?"

"Yes."

"You know where she went?"

"Yes."

"She told you?"

I heard her laugh bitterly. "She put a pencil mark around the ad for the place in the newspaper."

Lou wasn't a dumb one. I suspected she knew all about it from the beginning.

"I'm coming to get you," I said.

"You're not going to go after her?"

"Yes, but with you."

"I don't want to go."

"You know perfectly well you're going."

She said nothing so I went on.

"It'll be a lot easier if I take you away."

"But why go after her?"

"After all we've got to tell her."

"Tell her what?"

It was my turn to laugh.

"I'll remind you of that while we're riding. Now get your things ready and come along.

"Where should I wait for you."

"I'm just leaving. I'll be there in a couple of hours."

"With your car?"

"Yes. Wait in your room. I'll honk three times."

"I'll see."

"I'll be right over."

I didn't wait for her to answer, and hung up. I pulled out my handkerchief to wipe my forehead. I got out of the booth. The operator called me back for overtime. I paid and went back upstairs. I'd already put my stuff in the car, and had my money on me. I'd written a letter to the main office explaining that I had to leave suddenly to see a sick brother. Tom would forgive me that. I don't know what I expected to do with that bookstore job. It didn't worry me too much. I wasn't cutting anything much off from me. Until then I'd always been able to live without any trouble, and I'd never felt insecure in any way at all, but this business was beginning to get me wrought up and things weren't going as well as usual. I wished I was already down there to straighten out everything and get something else to do. I can't stand being in the middle of a job, and it was the same with this business. I looked around to make sure I hadn't forgotten anything. I picked up my hat, went out and locked the door. I kept the key. My car was waiting for me a block away. I turned the ignition and took off. As soon as I was out of town, I stepped hard on the gas and let her ride.

XVIII

It was damn dark on the highway, and I was glad there wasn't too much traffic. Mostly trucks, going the other way. Nobody much going my way. I let her rip. The motor roared like a tractor and the thermometer was way up around two hundred, but I pushed her all the same and she stood up.

I just wanted to calm down. After about an hour of that racket I felt better and I slowed down to the point where I could hear some of the other noises of the chassis.

The night was cold and somewhat damp. You could feel that winter was coming, but I left my coat in my valise. Lord, I can't remember when I ever felt warmer. I watched the road-signs, but the road wasn't complicated. Every now and then I passed a gas-station or a row of shacks, and then just the road. Sometimes an animal scooted across the road, and I passed plots of fruit trees and some wheat fields, or nothing at all.

I figured on two to cover the hundred miles. As a matter of fact, it was really a hundred and eight or nine, not counting the time lost getting out of Buckton and riding around their grounds when I got there. I was out at Lou's place in an hour and a half, or maybe a minute more. I'd asked the car for all it could give. I think Lou must have been ready so I slowed down almost to a stop passing the gate. I got as close to the house as possible and I pressed the horn-button three times. At first I didn't hear a thing. I couldn't see her window from where I was, but I didn't dare get out, and I didn't want to honk again lest I rouse up somebody.

I just sat there and waited, and I saw that my hands were trembling when I lit a cigarette to calm my nerves. I threw it away a couple of minutes later and then I hesitated as to whether I should signal again with my horn. And then, just as I was about to get out, I felt that she was on her way, and I turned around and saw her coming up to the car.

She had on a light coat, didn't have any hat, and carried a big leather handbag which looked as though it was going to bust, and nothing else. She got in and sat down next to me without saying a word. I closed the door bending over her, but I didn't try to kiss her. She was as cold as an icicle.

I took off and turned around to get back on the highway. She stared at the road straight ahead of her. I looked at her out of the corner of my eye and I thought that once we had gotten out of town things ought to go better. I did another hundred miles at top speed. We began to feel that we were getting there. The air was drier and the sky was brighter. I still had another five or six hundred miles to go.

I couldn't keep on sitting beside her and just say nothing. Besides her perfume had filled the car. In a way it got me terribly excited, since it brought back to mind the picture of her standing in her bedroom with her torn panties and lynx eyes. I heaved a loud sigh so she'd notice it. She seemed to sort of wake up, to come back to life sort of, and I tried to create a more cordial atmosphere—her chilliness still bothered me.

"Cold?"

"No," she said.

She shivered, and that made her even madder. I decided she was trying to put on an act of jealousy, but I was too busy driving to try to do much about it, that is by talking, especially if she continued to be so unresponsive. I let go the wheel with my right hand and bent over to the glove compartment. I dug out a bottle of whiskey and laid it in her lap. I also found a bakelite cup there. I put that in her lap next to the bottle, shut the glove compartment and then switched on the radio.

I should have thought of that earlier, but I was too wrought up.

What bothered me was the thought that I still had the whole job to pull off. Fortunately she took the bottle, screwed off the cap, poured herself a shot and tossed it down. I stretched out my hand. She filled the glass again and drained it herself. Only then did she pour one for me. I didn't even taste what I was drinking and I gave her back the glass. She put everything back into the glove compartment, stretched herself out on the seat and unbuttoned the two big buttons on her coat. She was wearing a suit with a short skirt and long coat-lapels. She unbuttoned the jacket too. Underneath she had on a lemon colored sweater right on her skin and for safety's sake, I forced myself to look at the road.

The car now smelt of perfume and whiskey and cigarette smoke, a combination that made my head reel. I didn't open the windows however. We maintained our silence. At least a half an hour went by. Then she opened up the glove compartment again and had a couple of more drinks. She felt hot now and took off her coat. As she did it, and came close to me, I bent over a little and kissed her neck, just below the ear. She jerked away suddenly and turned around and stared at me. And

then she burst into laughter. I guess the
whiskey was beginning to take effect. I drove
another fifty miles without saying anything,
and then I decided to try again. She'd had
some more drinks.

"Don't feel right?"

"Good enough," she said in a drawl.

"Don't feel like going out with me, do
you?"

"Oh, don't mind."

"Don't feel like seeing your darling sister?"

"Don't talk to me about my sister."

"She's a nice girl."

"Yeah, and she's good to screw, isn't
she?"

That took my breath away. If any of the
others had said that I'd hardly have noticed,
Judy, B.J, or Jicky. But not Lou. She saw I was
startled and laughed until I thought she'd
choke. You could see she'd been drinking
from the way she laughed.

"Isn't that the way you say it?"

"Yes," I agreed. "That's it, alright."

"And isn't that what she does?"

"I don't know."

She laughed again.

"It's no use, Lee. I'm too old to believe
that you get yourself a baby by kissing some

body on the mouth."

"Who said anything about a baby?"

"Jean is going to have a baby."

"Are you sick or something?"

"There's no sense lying to me, Lee. I know all about it."

"I didn't sleep with your sister."

"Yes you did."

"I didn't. And even if I had, she isn't going to have any baby."

"Why is she sick all the time?"

"She was sick at Jicky's house, and after all, she didn't have a baby then. You sister's got a delicate stomach."

"And what about the rest of her? That isn't too delicate, is it?"

Then she suddenly unleashed on me a hail of blows with her fists. I pulled my head back into my shoulders and I stepped on the gas. She hit down at me with all her strength. It wasn't much but I felt it all the same. She didn't have much muscles, but she had the strength of her anger. And then she'd gotten plenty of build up playing tennis. When she stopped I just shook myself.

"Do you feel better now."

"I feel swell. Did Jean feel better afterwards?"

"After what?"

"After you screwed her?"

She sure must have gotten a big kick out of saying that word. If I'd put my fingers between her legs I'm sure I would have had to wipe them afterwards.

"Oh," I said, "that wasn't the first time for her."

Again a hail of blows.

"You're a filthy liar, Lee Anderson."

She was panting from the effort and stared at the road again.

"I think I'd rather screw you,' I said. "I like the way you smell better, and you've got more hair on your belly. But Jean isn't bad. I'll miss it with her once we're rid of her."

She didn't move. She took that blow without flinching. My throat was parched and at that instant I got a sudden flash of understanding. I thought I realized what she felt.

"Are we going to do it right away," she murmured, "or only afterwards?"

"Do what?" I said in a low voice.

I could hardly speak.

"Are you going to screw me?" she said in such a low voice. I felt rather than heard what she had said.

I was now as excited as a bull, it almost hurt.

"We've got to get rid of her first," I said.

I said that only to see if she was really hooked.

"I don't want to," she said.

"You really care that much for your sister? You don't want to go the whole way?"

"No, not that, I don't want to wait."

Luckily for me, I saw a gas station and stopped the car. I had to get my mind on something else, otherwise I might lose my head. I didn't get out, but just told the guy to fill her up. Lou twisted the door-handle and got out. She asked the man something in a low voice, and he pointed out a shack to her. She went in and came back in about ten minutes. I took advantage of the break to put some air in a soft tire and to get the guy to bring me a sandwich that I couldn't get myself to eat.

Lou got back in. I'd paid the mechanic, and he went back to bed. I started the car and drove at full throttle again for a couple of hours. Lou didn't stir. She looked as though she were sleeping. I'd calmed myself down to normal. All of a sudden she straightened up and opened the glove compartment again, and sent down three drinks, one after the other.

I couldn't watch her move any more without my getting all excited. I tried to keep driving, but a couple of miles farther up I stopped the car on the shoulder. It was still dark. However, you could feel that dawn was coming. There was no wind at all. Nothing but clusters of trees and bushes all around. We hadn't gone through a town for almost a half hour.

After I'd set the brakes, I took the bottle and drank a shot, and then I told her to get out. She opened the door and took her bag, and I followed her. She went over the trees and stopped when we got there and asked me for a cigarette. I'd left them in the car. I told her to wait. She started rummaging in her bag to look for some but I'd already taken off. I ran to the car. I took the bottle back too. It was almost empty, but I had more in the trunk in the rear.

Coming back I could hardly walk comfortably, and I started unbuttoning my fly before I reached her. I suddenly saw the flash of a revolver shot, and at the same instant I felt as though my left elbow explode. My arm fell limp at my side. If I hadn't been twisted up fixing my pants I probably would have gotten the slug in my chest.

That all passed through my head in a second. And a second later I was on top of her and was twisting her wrist and then I gave her a heavy blow across her forehead with all my strength, because she had tried to bite me. I was in a bad position and it hurt like hell. She caught my blow and fell to the ground, motionless. I wasn't ready for that yet. I picked up the gun and put it in my pocket. It was a little pea-shooter like mine, but she had aimed right. I ran back to the car. I held my left arm with my right hand and I must have had a face like a Chinese mask, but I was so mad I hardly noticed how much it hurt.

I found what I was looking for, some rope, and I went back. Lou had begun to move. I had a hard time tying up her arms with only one hand. When I had her trussed up I began to slap her; I tore off her skirt and ripped her sweater and then went back to slapping her. I held her down with my knee while I tried to get her damn sweater off, but I only managed to rip open the front. It began to get light in the eastern sky; part of her body was right in the deepest shadow of the tree.

She then tried to talk and she told me I wouldn't have her because she had just telephoned to Dex to tell the police and she thought I was a horrible monster ever since I'd talked about getting rid of her sister. I laughed and I slugged her jaw with my fist because she seemed to be smiling too. Her chest was cold and hard. I asked her why she had shot me and I tried hard to control myself when she called me a dirty nigger and said that Dexter had told her that, and that she had come with me to warn Jean, and that she hated me more than anybody in her whole life.

I laughed again. I felt my heart pounding like a trip hammer, my hands were trembling and my left arm was still bleeding hard; I felt the blood run down my forearm.

Then I told her that white men had killed my brother and that they'd have a tough time getting me and that she was going to die in any case and I squeezed one of her breasts until she almost fainted, but she didn't cry out. I slapped her again with all my strength.

She opened her eyes again. The sun was going to rise soon. I could see her eyes shine with tears and with hatred. I bent over her. I think I must have snorted and panted like a wild beast and she began to scream. I bit her right between the thighs. I had my mouth full of black stiff hairs. I opened my jaws and clenched them again a little farther down where it was softer. I was dizzy with her perfume,—she had plenty of it there, and I closed my teeth tighter. I tried to put my hand on her mouth, but she squealed like a stuck pig, blood curdling cries. I bit harder, with all my strength and I cut through the flesh. I felt the blood gush into my mouth and her body writhed in spite of the rope. My face was smeared with blood and I sat back on my haunches a bit. I'd never heard a woman scream like that; all of a sudden I felt that I was shooting off in my shorts. It effected me stronger than any other time in my life, but I was afraid somebody would come.

I struck a match and saw that she was bleeding hard. Finally I began to hit down again, at first just with my right fist on her jaw, I felt her teeth shatter but I kept it up, I wanted her to stop screaming. I hit harder and then I lifted her skirt and stuck it over her mouth and then I sat down on her head. She still wriggled like an eel. I didn't think she would have held on to life so hard. She thrashed about so violently I thought my left forearm would be jerked off. I now felt such a rage that I could have skinned her alive. I got up to finish her off with some kicks. Finally I put my foot across her throat and put all my weight on it. When she had stopped moving, I felt myself go off a second time. I now felt my knees trembling and was afraid that I would faint.

XIX

I should have gone after the pick and shovel and buried her there, but I was afraid of the cops now. I didn't want to be caught before I'd taken care of Jean. I felt the kid point the way to me. I knelt down beside Lou. I untied the rope that held her hands. There were deep cuts on her wrists and she felt soft and flabby, like corpses that are still warm. Her breasts were losing their shape. I didn't pull the skirt down off her face. I didn't want to see her head any more. I took her watch however. I wanted to have something of hers.

I suddenly thought of how my face must look and I ran back to the car. When I looked in the mirror I saw there wasn't too much to fix up. I washed myself with a little whiskey. My arms had stopped bleeding. I managed to get it out of my sleeve and tie it tight against my body with my scarf and some rope. I almost howled, it hurt so much when I bent it back. I managed, especially after I'd gotten another bottle out of the trunk. I guess I'd lost a lot of time—the sun was almost on the horizon. I took Lou's coat out of the car and draped it over her,—I didn't want

to drag it around with me. I couldn't feel my
legs any more, but my hands weren't trembling so bad any more.

I got back in behind the wheel and started the car. I wondered what she could have
told Dex. Her story about the cops began to
bother me, but I didn't really think about it. It
just stayed in the back of my mind, like an
echo.

I now wanted to take care of Jean and
feel again what I'd felt twice while I was wip-
ing out her sister. I found what I'd always
been looking for. The thought of the cops
bothered me, but still only vaguely—that
wouldn't stop me from doing what I wanted to
do,—I'd gone too far. They'd have to go
damn fast to catch up with me. I still had
about three hundred miles to do. My left arm
was beginning to get numb, and I sent the gas-
pedal all the way down.

XX

I began to remember lots of things about an hour before I got there. I remembered the day I'd gotten my hands on a guitar for the fist time. It was at a neighbor's house, he gave me some lessons secretly. I practiced only one song, "When the Saints go Marching On" and I learned to play and sing the whole thing together with the chorus.

One evening I borrowed the neighbor's guitar to surprise everybody at home; Tom sang with me and the kid acted like he was crazy, dancing around the table as though he was leading a parade; he took a stick and twirled it about. Just then my pop came in and he laughed and sang with us. I took the guitar back to the neighbor, but next day I found one on my bed; a second-hand one, but a good one. Everyday I practiced a little. The guitar is a lazy man's instrument. You pick it up, strum out a tune and then you drop it, laze around, pick it up again to strike a couple of chords to accompany yourself while whistling some tune. The days go by quickly that way.

I snapped out of it suddenly when I hit a bump on the road. I think I almost fell

asleep. I hardly felt my left arm anymore and I
was parched with thirst. I tried to think back to
the good old days just to get my mind off
things, because I was so impatient to get there
that whenever I started thinking about it I felt
my heart pound against my ribs and my right
hand tremble on the wheel. I had a lot of trouble driving with just one hand. I wondered
what Tom would do if he were in my place; he
was probably praying now back in his school.
From Tom my mind traveled to Clem, and
then to Buckton, where I stayed three months
running a book-store and earning a good living. I remembered Jicky and the time I'd
screwed her in the water, and how clear the
stream was that day. Jicky so young, smooth,
naked, like a baby, and all of a sudden that
made me think of Lou and her black muff,
thick and curly, and of the taste I had in my
mouth when I bit it, a sweetish, salty taste, hot,
and the smell of perfume from her thighs; ;and
I again heard her screams in my ear. I felt the
sweat run down my forehead and I couldn't let
go the damn wheel to wipe it.

My stomach felt as though it was all
swollen up with gas and pushed on my
diaphragm crushing my lungs and Lou
screamed in my ears. I reached over to the center horn-button, on the wheel, I had an extra

set of horns on the car and I pressed everything down at once to drown out her screams.

I must have been doing about eighty-
five or so; the car couldn't do much better, but
then I started down a long grade and I saw the
needle edge over three, four more miles. The
sun had been up for some time. A lot of cars
went by in the other direction, and I passed
some on my side. After a couple of minutes I
let up on the horns, I was afraid to arouse
some motor-cycle-cops and I didn't have
enough speed to get away from them. When I
got there I'd take Jean's ear, but Lord, when
was I going to get there.

I think I began to squeal there in the car,
to squeal like a pig, with my teeth clenched, I
was able to go faster that way, and I took a
curve without slowing down with a horrible
shrieking of the tires. The Nash swung over
violently, but straightened up again after having cut over to the left shoulder and I kept the
accelerator pedal down to the floor and I
laughed happily like the kid when he danced
around the table singing "When the Saints Go
Marching On" and I almost wasn't afraid any
more.

XXI

That damn shivering came back on me anyhow, just before I got to the hotel. It was almost half past eleven. Jean must have expected me at breakfast as I had told her. I opened the door on the right and got out that side because with my arm it was easiest that way.

The hotel was a sort of white building in the local style with drawn blinds. They still had plenty of sun down there, even though it was towards the end of October. I didn't find a soul downstairs. It was nowhere near as nice a place as described in the ad, but as far as privacy, you couldn't have asked for anything better.

I counted about a dozen other shacks and a gas station and cafe a little off the road, probably a truck-stop... I went outside again. As I figured, the sleeping cabins ought to be separate from the hotel and I thought they might be up the path that led off at right angles to the road. There were some miserable trees about and some sparse grass. I left the car and went up the path. It turned not far up, and right after that I ran into Jean's car in front of a cabin with two fairly clean rooms. I went in without knocking.

She was sitting on an armchair and seemed to be sleeping. She didn't look so good, but still had on her swank clothes. I wanted to wake her up but the phone,—there was one in the cabin,—began to ring right then. I lost my head like a dope and jumped on it. My heart beat wildly again. I took off the receiver and slammed it back on. I knew that Dex was the only one who might call her. Dex or the cops. Jean rubbed her eyes. She got up and I kissed her right off, so hard she almost cried out. She felt wide awake now. I put my arm around her to lead her out. Just then she noticed my empty sleeve.

"What's the matter, Lee?"

She looked frightened. I laughed. It wasn't a nice laugh.

"It's nothing. I tripped like a dope getting out of the car and I smashed my elbow."

"But you've been bleeding."

"Just a scratch. Come on, Jean. I've had enough of that trip. I just want to be alone with you now."

The phone started ringing again and I felt as though the electric current had been stepped up through my body rather than going through the wires. I couldn't control myself and I grabbed it and threw it on the floor.

I broke it to bits with my heels. I suddenly felt as though I was crushing Lou's face again with my shoes. I broke out into a sweat, and I almost ran out. I know that my lips were trembling and I must have looked like a madman.

Fortunately Jean didn't press me. She went out and I told her to get into her car. We'd ride off a bit to be more alone and we'd come back for breakfast later. It was damn late for breakfast, but she seemed to be in a daze. Still sick, I guessed, because of the baby that was coming. I pressed on the gas pedal. The car jerked as I started it, throwing us back hard against the seat. It was almost all over now. Just hearing the motor calmed me. I said something to Jean to explain about the phone; she began to notice I was raving and I told myself it was about time for me to stop it. She snuggled against me and put her head on my shoulder.

I waited until we had covered about twenty miles, and then I looked for a good place to stop. I found a stretch where the road was built up on an embankment. I thought that we could just slide down the embankment and I could do it there. I stopped the car. She

got out first. I felt Lou's gun in my pocket. I
didn't want to use it right away. Even with
only one arm I could take care of Jean too. She
bent over to fix her shoe and I could see her
thighs under the short skirt that tightly mold-
ed her hips. I felt my mouth become dry. She
stopped near a bush. There was a spot there
where you couldn't see the road when you sat
down.

She stretched out on the ground. I took
her right there, but I didn't let myself go all the
way. I tried to keep myself calm, in spite of
her wriggling; I was able to make her go off
without having gone off myself. And then I
spoke to her.

"Do you always like it so much when
you get laid by a colored man?"

She didn't say a word. She looked para-
lyzed.

"You know, I've got more than an eighth
colored blood in me."

She opened her eyes again and I
laughed. She didn't know what was going on.
And then I told her everything : the whole
business of the kid, how he fell in love with a
girl and how her brother and father had taken
care of him; I told her what I wanted to do
with her and with Lou, to get double revenge.
I felt in my pocket and pulled out Lou's wrist-

watch. I showed it to her and then said I was sorry I hadn't been able to bring her one of her sister's eyes, but they were too poor condition after the special treatment I had given them.

It wasn't easy for me to say all that. The words didn't come out by themselves. She lay there on the ground, with her eyes closed and her skirt pushed up on her belly. I again felt that strange sensation that ran up my back and my hand closed on her throat and I couldn't stop myself; it came; it was so strong that I let her go and almost staggered to my feet. Her face was all blue, but she didn't move. She was still breathing I think. I took Lou's gun from my pocket and I sent two bullets into her neck, almost point-blank; the blood started bubbling out, slowly, in spurts, with a squirting sound. All you could see of her eyes was a white thread between her lids. She jerked suddenly, and I think that that was when she died. I turned her over so I wouldn't have to see her face any more, and while she was still warm I did to her just what I had done in her bedroom.

I think I must have fainted after that. When I came to, she was quite cold, and couldn't be stirred. I left her there and went up the bank to the car. I could hardly drag my feet; there were bright spots before my eyes; when I

was back behind the wheel I remembered that
the whiskey was back in the Nash and my
hand began trembling again.

XXII

Sergeant Culloughs put his pipe down on the desk.

"We'll never be able to stop him," he said.

Carter shook his head.

"We can try."

"You can't stop a man doing a hundred miles an hour in a light car like that with nothing but a couple of motor-cycles!"

"We can try. Might break our necks, but we can try."

Borrow still hadn't said anything. He was a big, sprawling fellow, somewhat dark, and he spoke with a drawl.

"I'm for it," he said.

"What do you say?" Carter asked.

Culloughs looked at them.

"Fellows," he said, "You might break your necks, but if you make it you can be sure of a promotion."

"After all you can't let a damn nigger turn the damn country upside down like that," Carter said.

Culloughs didn't reply, but looked at his watch.

"It's five o'clock," he said. "They called about ten minutes ago. He ought to go by in about five minutes. If he does go by."

"He killed two white girls," Carter said.

"And a mechanic," Barrow added.

He checked the 45 in the holster at his side and went to the door.

"There are some others hot on this trail," Culloughs said.

"According to the last report, they're still there. The headquarters staff car is after him, and they expect another too."

"I think we'd better get going," Carter said.

"Get on behind me," he said to Barrow. "We'll take only one bike."

"That isn't according to regulations," the sergeant objected.

"Borrow's a dead shot," Carter said. "But when you've got to drive the bike too, you can't shoot your best."

"Oh, do as you damn please." Culloughs said. "I wash my hands of the whole business.

The powerful motor-bike took off with a jerk. Barrow who was hooked onto Carter almost lifted him out of his seat. He was sitting backwards, back to back against Carter. The two of them were tied together by a leather belt.

"Slow down as soon as you get out of town," Barrow said.

"It isn't according to regulations," Culloughs grumbled at the same instant, as he watched Borrow's bike gloomily.

He shrugged his shoulders and went back into the police station. He went out almost right away and watched the big cream-colored Buick flash by with a roar of its motor. And then he heard the sirens and saw four motorcycles go by—so there were four of them after all—and then a police car right behind them.

"Damn lousy road," Culloughs grumbled again.

He didn't go back in.

He heard the sound of the sirens fade slowly away.

XXIII

Lee moved his jaws dryly. His right
hand shifted about nervously on the wheel
and he pressed down on the gas pedal with all
the weight of his body. His eyes were blood-
shot and the sweat streamed down his face.
His blond hair was matted with sweat and
dust. He could hardly hear the scream of the
sirens behind him even when he listened for it,
and the road was too poor for them to shoot at
him from that distance. He noticed a motor-
cycle just in front of him and he swerved to the
left to pass it, but it kept pacing him.
Suddenly the wind-shield was pierced by a
missile and he caught a shower of splintered
glass right in his face. The motor-cycle was
motionless relative to the Buick and Barrow
was able to take as careful aim as at the firing
range. Lee saw the flashes of the second and
third shots, but the bullets missed him. He
was now doing his best to zigzag about on the
road to duck the shots, but the wind-shield
shattered again, and even closer to his face.
He now felt the strong draft through the perfectly round hole the big metal .45 slug had cut
through.

And then he felt as though the Buick

was speeding up because he was getting closer to the bike, but he suddenly realized that the cops were slowing up. His lips formed a peculiar smile as he slowly decreased the pressure of his foot on the gas pedal. There was now no more than fifty feet between the two vehicles, forty, thirty... Lee suddenly pressed down hard again. He saw Barrows face just beside him and jerked violently under the blow of the bullet which hit his right shoulder. He passed the motorcycle grinding his teeth together so as not to let go the wheel. Once ahead of them he was out of the soup.

The road suddenly took a sharp curve, and then straightened out again. Carter and Barrow were still hot on his heel. In spite of the car springs, he felt every little bump in his injured arms. He looked into the rear-view mirror. Nothing had come around the curve yet besides the two men on the bike, and he then saw Carter slow down and stop on the shoulder to let Barrow turn around and get back on again since they weren't going to chance passing him by.

The road came to a fork a couple of hundred feet up. Lee noticed some sort of building to the right. Without letting up on the gas, he turned into the plowed-up field bordered by the dirt road to the right. The

Buick bounced way off the ground and almost twisted over, but righted itself again to the groaning complaint of all the car parts, and came to a halt before a barn. He got to the door. Both his arms were hurting like the devil. He felt the blood begin surging through his numb left arm again—it was still tied to his chest—and it forced moans of pain through his lips. He ran towards a wooden ladder that led up to the grain shed and he flung himself on its rungs. He almost lost his balance but regained it with a grotesquely contorted movement of his body and he took the fat, rough, wooden rungs between his teeth. He stopped halfway up, panting heavily, and a silver cut his lip. He felt how hard he was clenching his teeth together when he again felt in his mouth the salty taste of warm blood, as warm as he'd drunk from Lou's body, between her thighs smelling of a Paris perfume that was intended for a woman much older than her. He again saw Lou's twisted mouth and the skirt of her suit smeared with blood and again there were bright flashes before this eyes.

Slowly, painfully, he struggled up several more rungs as the scream of the sirens came closer. Lou's screams mixed in with the noise of the sirens, and the whole scene flashed vividly in his brain, he began to kill Lou all

over again, and the same sensation, the same
surge of pleasure shook him again as he
reached the flooring of the grain-shed. The
noise had died down outside the barn. Inch by
inch, he pulled himself up to the little window.
He couldn't use his right arm at all now
because the slightest movement brought it
excruciating pain.

Before him, as far as he could see, the
yellow fields stretched out monotonously. The
sun was going down, and a slight breeze was
waving the grass along the edge of the road.
The blood ran down his right sleeve and his
body. He was slowly exhausting his last bit of
strength, and he began to tremble with fear
again.

The cops had completely surrounded
the barn by now. He heard them call to him,
and he opened his mouth wide, but soundless-
ly. He was thirsty and he was sweaty and he
wanted to shout defiance and insults at them,
but his throat was too parched. He watched
his blood make a little puddle near him and
finally run over and soak into his knee. He
trembled like a leaf in the wind, and his teeth
chattered, and when he heard steps on the ladder he began to bawl, a low moan at first
which grew and swelled into a mad bellow; he
tried to get the revolver out of his pocket, and

finally got it at the cost of almost unbearable pain. He flattened his body against the wall, as far away as possible from the opening in the floor the cops would climb through. He held the gun in his hand, but he couldn't shoot.

The noise had stopped completely now. He stopped bellowing and his head fell back on his chest. He heard some vague sounds. Some time passed, and then several bullets struck him in the hip.

His body relaxed and slowly flowed to the floor. A thread of saliva stretched from his mouth to the coarse boards of the barn floor. The rope with which he'd slung up his left arm had left deep glue cuts in his flesh.

XXIV

The townspeople hanged him anyway because he was a nigger. Under his trousers, his crotch still protruded ridiculously.